About the Author

Jan Van Aken (1971) is a Belgian (Flemish) author. 'Wytham Whales' is his fourth, but first English novel (no translation). His other Dutch titles are 'De Waterdief' (2015), 'Kwien of the fleas' (2017) and 'Phossils koffer' (2021). Van Aken is a language teacher (Dutch, English and German) in Antwerp, a cherished cook at home and an anglophile in heart and soul.

Wytham Whales

Jan Van Aken

Wytham Whales

Vanguard Press

VANGUARD PAPERBACK

© Copyright 2024 **Jan Van Aken**
Illustrations © Jan Van Aken 2019

The right of Jan Van Aken to be identified as author of
this work has been asserted by him in accordance with the
Copyright, Designs and Patents Act 1988.

All Rights Reserved

No reproduction, copy or transmission of this publication
may be made without written permission.
No paragraph of this publication may be reproduced,
copied or transmitted save with the written permission of the
publisher, or in accordance with the provisions
of the Copyright Act 1956 (as amended).

Any person who commits any unauthorised act in relation to
this publication may be liable to criminal
prosecution and civil claims for damages.

A CIP catalogue record for this title is
available from the British Library.

ISBN 978 1 83794 216 9

This is a work of fiction. Names, characters, businesses, places, events and
incidents are either the product of the author's imagination or used in a
fictitious manner. Any resemblance to actual persons, living or dead, or actual
events is purely coincidental.

*Vanguard Press is an imprint of
Pegasus Elliot Mackenzie Publishers Ltd.*
www.pegasuspublishers.com

First Published in 2024

**Vanguard Press
Sheraton House Castle Park
Cambridge England**

Printed & Bound in Great Britain

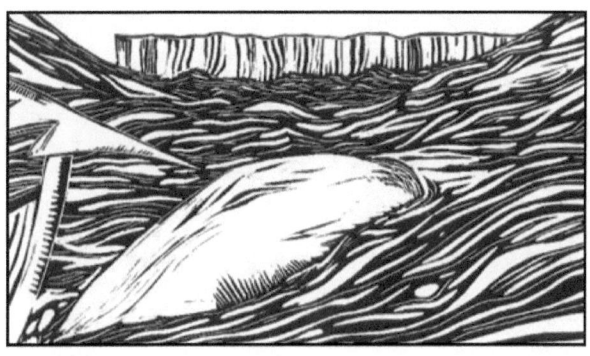

'*He piled upon the whale's white hump the sum of all the general rage and hate felt by his whole race from Adam down; and then, as if his chest had been a mortar, he burst his hot heart's shell upon it.*'
  'Moby Dick' by H. Melville (1819-1891)

PROLOGUE

The water does what it actually has been doing for the last couple of years. Taking land relentlessly. Inch by inch. At first, it looked innocent, but gradually it got nastier, when personal borders were being pushed uphill. It pulls people out of their deadening comfort zones and turns them into fierce competitors, like an outlived couple that struggles with a downsized bed overnight. They cling desperately to what is already mouldy and wet.

It reminds me of Brexit, which had a similar aspiration, the same poor ambition of salvation. It had redefined the land as well. Not by rising water levels, like it is doing now, but by imposing the same sort of distinct borders.

The idea of being trapped by unforgiving frontiers always evokes primal ethics and politics. We have become survivors, landwrecked survivors. Indigenous castaways, if you like.

ACT I

Burial

'Shouldn't we inform the continent?'

David sweeps the table surface with his left hand and clears the spilled food in his other, scuffing my notebook deliberately with the rancid smelling cloth, making everything more appalling than it already is.

David can't have it. Work and food on the very same spot, at least when an indoor kitchen table is involved, which is weird, I think.

Frankly, there's something paradoxical about this place. Like a tiled flushing toilet in the middle of a jungle or an abandoned but connected overgrown red phone booth.

David's so called working space for instance lies at the southeast edge of the woods. An improvised row of ruinous open sheds in a field, each sheltering a Japanese kiln. They were built after some ancient traditional Anagama models, but exposed to the relentless elements of Nature. Since a badly stocked gas bottle took the life of their founder, that same Nature has regained positions frighteningly easily. The symptoms of abandonment quickly showed once the hymns had died. The rewilding has already put two of the three kiln dragons down. Departments still exchange reproaches about the lack of proper storing facilities, while perhaps worst of all, previously assigned renovation funds have suddenly vanished into the thinnest of airs. The loyal foresters keep delivering chopped wood though, because of an ironic abundance. David is grateful for that, but every year more miracles and magic are needed to get the site operational again.

There are numerous examples of lost or unfinished sieges of the Hill. Starting perhaps from the silent Hill End camp site and Hazel's scattered innocent swimming pools, over the silted trenches on the other side of the woods, up to the much later decisive installation of the fieldwork headquarters in the grand chalet, the old dismantled, transported and rebuilt Swiss hunting lodge on the hilltop from the 1930s.

Since the woods were bequeathed to the university, our kind sneaked up the hill like a whipped up Roman legion. Keen academics with nervous endeavours, multiplying the human diversity in the woods with aspirational presence. Merely foot soldiers. Some driven by ambition, some by greed, one alternatively more pushing than the other, to count, measure, map and face the degenerating wildlife under the partly industrially planted timber of Wytham Woods. And we all cherish the delicate hope of triumph in that High Street parade of the academic universe, backed by a scholar who is holding homegrown laurels above our squeezed heads, whispering enviously that our lonely partners hardly resist the ubiquitous advances in town. The rising levels now only just reconfirm the massive circles we constantly fail to square.

As said, it's a small miracle David got that last dragon loaded and burning. He is all tensed up. There is a brutal urge in his movements since he stubbornly decided to start the firing anyway. All by himself, after the rest of his team had left to roll up carpets and save kittens. I secretly hoped it would render hopeful perspectives to his fading craft, but again, it now feels more like a hot-brained battle he had already lost before he even started. That was two days ago. He's most likely too affronted to give in, let alone to beg again for any assistance since we all refused blatantly to volunteer one single shift under these least inviting weather conditions. He surprised us with an unexpected hasty nutritional visit, before that last stretch of his seventy-two-hour marathon of soothing the insatiable hunger of a raging dragon with nicely chopped beech, oak and birch. Nature is playing a cruel game and we don't seem to surrender.

David is a Welsh potter from Holyhead, Anglesey. Every year, he exchanges the wide sea view for an enclosed woodland scenery and claims Wytham's kiln site during the whole summer recess. He's a chunky young man who thinks like a steaming locomotive. Straightforward and once set off, hardly unstoppable. A trait that suits flame taming hobbies, I guess, but I give in like wet moulded clay whenever he approaches. Frankly, he is modesty itself. It's actually only me, who organically inclines.

David usually gets most of the attention, even though he never seeks it. The few invasive tourist permit holder families normally venture the equally modest summit, and sneak in under the open sheds to ask him the most awkward questions with a rather lazy, feigned scientific interest, considering their poor persistence to digest the elaborated answers that follow. The children soon regret their parents' question. It feels like they've opened Pandora's box. You cannot imagine how many ideas and figures David has been chewing on, while throwing clay above his lonely Welsh spinning wheel during even lonelier Welsh winter days. His words had enough time to dry and hardened by the salty spring breezes that are stroking Mona Island. They seem ready to convert the nescient, empty-headed yuppies, the poor sort who lost touch with Nature, resources, tools and materials. The whole family give in remorsefully, having the kids join in some sort of artisanal, messy workshop. The proof lies in their content descent of the hill, loaded with the weirdest knobbly mugs or cups, cheaply wrapped in even more cheap brown paper. Different from any tableware in the shops, but loyally bought for some quid to re-earth their detached soul and to cover David's incurred costs of London clay and maintenance. The visitors look somewhat purged after all, although still clay spotted on places where the itches persist.

According to David's rhetoric, the kiln is an ancient, archetypal way of bringing people together. There's this unique communal, non-hierarchical feel to it, triggered by the creating force of fire and the modest role man is granted in this fascinating natural process. You're never able to handle the four elements completely, I once heard David humbly confess to a group of middle-aged spinsters from Saint Hilda's, even though we're fortunate to play with them. We're just keepers, modest keepers, and there's no fame to gain whatsoever. Most female permit holders adore him. They picture him as a druid, a master of the elements, from water and clay, to fire and air. Perhaps that's why he awkwardly favours at least one cleared dinner surface here in the chalet.

I do moths, by the way. Night moths. Invisible to common people, as they mostly appear when they drink, flirt, wank, shag or sleep. And I do none of them, apart from wanking and sleeping.

'Do you mean Europe?'

Alan turns his head while rinsing a last plate under the running tap. His other arm disappears in murky dishwater. It has been his turn since the beginning of the week, but he has always weaselled out when duty called. Being a marine biologist, the rising water level evoked an urgency in his eel project, as his field of research has been expanding drastically over the weeks. It is in a way the only habitat that has sneaked in brutally on the observer's domain, rather than the other way around. One of the reasons why smart Alan once took up marine biology, I guess, the rising sea levels.

Fortunately, Wytham Hill still rises safely up from the flooded Isis valley, but has lost the last dry link with its vital instructive urban base called Oxford about two weeks ago. In this post-Brexit era, it's pretty tricky to think in terms of islands and continents. These newly installed networks of dependencies are getting quite confusing. Anyway, the legion has been cut off and fresh supplies are running short.

'No, the university,' David replies. 'It's no use staying much longer after tomorrow.'

Read David doesn't win anything with staying. His clay collection will have reached its aimed glazing temperature by tomorrow morning, and afterwards, there's nothing exciting about a natural cooling process, which normally takes twice as long. You usually have a drink or a fag if you can't kick off from the smoke and you return to a normal life back in town if you've led any.

'You should use more soap. There are seven of us. And the plates were greasy enough to justify the spillage of amines rather than five gallons of clear water.'

Aoife is bad at estimating. Especially when agitated. She exaggerates easily in any direction thinkable. As long as it suits her. Not a very scientific mindset, I reckon, but one cannot always have the saucepan on the academic stove, she defends.

'There's plenty of water outside, love, don't panic,' reassures Alan.

Aoife loathes being addressed that way. It reminds her of her Sudanese ex-boyfriend who thought he could treat women the same way here as he did in his country.

Alan does it deliberately as well, but less exposed. I just know. As David did with the dishcloth. Alpha male behaviour, to affirm the hierarchy in the hill pack. The borders of our artificial island are constantly being defied. Habitats are running out and the call of science gets overruled by friction and emotions. We sometimes look like a group of bonobos in an abandoned zoo. Luckily, time still brings solace since the evening meal is, so far, the only inevitable, tricky shared moment left. The silences at the table get embarrassing and unpleasant.

The other day, Georg suddenly stated the rainfall had turned us into sworn in MPs of the hill. We have full control now, he claimed, because nobody else can tell us what to do, or even better, not to do. Mr. Lyndon, Wytham's official chalet custodian, left the island to bring his cats and chickens into safety. He was the last official thread of nosy authority. So...

Nobody openly replied to Georg's weird political statement, but surely everybody contemplated on the power vacuum that has been created and the retired ambitions it might have awoken. At least I did. But I didn't get any further than breaking into Mr Lyndon's West-Vleteren collection. I once smuggled two wooden crates for him into the country. I don't think the man has ever fully realised what precious liquid gold that poorly working cellar hatch was hiding. I honestly saved it from drowning and gave it a more purposeful ending than pointless drainage. He should be most grateful for that, I believe.

It annoyed everybody that Boris was occupied with his mobile throughout the whole supper. Only to secure an obscure trade of a big enough amount of Bitcoins to legitimise the breaking of the only remaining house rule since the flooding started apparently. Aoife once fancied Boris for his wealth. I say fancied because she quickly realised that she would never get herself between him and his offshore bank accounts. How enormous these distances even might be. He never talks about his solvency openly, but his characteristic phlegm seems to be built on numbers. Mostly positive ones, of course. The major difference with maths students, he mocks. He even laughs at David's medieval looking workshops shaped into some fragile business model the university yearly claims in order to grant him the permit for his annual firing projects.

Boris himself is completely independent, even self-sufficient. That aura of self-indulgence at such a young age might have triggered Aoife too. I still keep wondering what on earth would have turned her on in that short, upcoming bank manager-like character. He is the smallest of the men, but the heaviest in wealth and weight. He reads modern history, but clearly aims at foreign diplomacy. Nobody really knows what brought him to Wytham Hill. The sort of conscientious objector, sticking to the military metaphor, if you like. He says he needs the woods to outweigh the temptations of modern life and to hide from the nasty tentacles of town. Weirdly enough, he is still the most connected person of us all. Even now, when we're isolated.

'No, I mean David is right,' Boris agrees. 'I even think we should consider a genuine evacuation plan ourselves. Eventually. Perhaps. Next week's weather forecast is anything but reassuring.'

I spot a hint of doubt. Most likely inspired by some worrying financial feeds from yonder side. Boris likes full control and whenever some checks wear out, he starts freaking out. It's really a miracle he's still with us, in this relentless realm of raging currents. I go for miscalculated speculations. Even he seems not indefectible.

'What do you mean?' says Georg. 'Abandon ship? The engines are running fine. Why leave? Just for once no sneaky eyes.'

Georg throws his words in when he is about to leave the room first. That's his way of debating. He simply backs off, whenever he suspects a looming issue behind his seemingly cloudless horizons. Georg counts the twelve recently introduced sleeping hazel dormice, muscardinus avellanarius. I know their Latin name because we sometimes cross each other's field of interest. Hardly impossible not to on this godforsaken tied up hilltop. I even suspect them for eating my flying friends, at whatever vulnerable crawling stage of life they're in. A sensitive topic that is better left untouched as we both consider ourselves victims of that bigger evil which one would bluntly call extinction.

'I agree,' shouts Elizabeth to an empty doorway, lazily filtering the streams of secondary info from behind her mushroom book. 'The cargo is too precious to be neglected.'

I always look up when Elizabeth speaks. Every excuse is fine to look at her. She's displayed herself lazily on the settee, with only a long cardigan covering her rangy white upper thighs and a book she has professionally positioned in her lap. It is a general but unspoken rule of the hill to milk a mooted metaphor in the extreme. Till the mental game leads the conversation too far off the subject. Vanity corrupts. And that's all there is to it.

I plunge into my notebook again and close my eyes to frame Elizabeth's legs in my memory. She is right about the swift course the boat is taking. All is going well, apart from the weather and our infantile malarkey we allow ourselves into. David wrings the dishcloth under the running tap and drops the rag in the filthy water again, the silly devil. The solitary marathon clearly takes its toll.

'Why this sudden worry over sovereignty issues,' Elizabeth remarks sharply, 'when my flags are being moved every single day?'

'I'm innocent. I didn't do any of it, you know that,' Georg immediately denies, but rather cheaply to be honest. His Russian accent doesn't help him much either, especially when Elizabeth has drawn some nasty parallels with Putin's brutal invasion of Ukraine. These barbaric flag incidents could only have been prompted by envy. Why else would one insistingly keep moving coloured field markings? This was not just an accidental repairing guesswork of embarrassingly relocating flags on some half-plundered French cheese plate. This mischievous behaviour was undoubtedly triggered by a clear motive, though, defining it, seems more delicate and challenging than her research on fungi networks on a degenerating tree trunk. Bringing up this other sensitive topic only means the case hasn't been closed at all. Like many things on the hilltop. They surface, now and again, and then disappear for days or decades.

'I'm not accusing anyone,' Elizabeth finishes firmly, 'I was just surprised by this sudden rehabilitation of ethics, that's all.'

Another silence follows. Like an uncomfortable void of mental distancing, which frankly has only intensified after the new water lockdown. Like I said, this is a weird place to live.

'So, what shall we do then, Bernie?' Alan suddenly poses, distracting the conversation from one of the many gnawing mysteries of the hill.

Eventually, when all other battlegrounds have been trodden, they get finally after me, with a scornful pathetic French accent to mock my Belgian background, even though I'm from the northern part of the country. I also feel being spiked with a wrong coloured flag. They all look at me, apart from Elizabeth. Thank God. But I seem targeted by an allied teasing to get some crucial state of the hill union out of my mouth. Even Georg pops his head back in.

There's another silence, but now for the seventh and final opinion that should balance out any built up rivalry. I weigh the mocking in the men's instant interest in my semi-autistic insights and I sense the flaw of it all, certainly when Elizabeth keeps on reading.

'I think we'd better stay and do what we're expected to do. I don't see any reason why we should interrupt our observations. The problems will be the same elsewhere, probably even worse. As long as there is food, drinkable water and electricity to charge my batteries, I stay.'

Sounds erupt out of my mouth, like a volcanic explosion. Hard-boiled words stream in rapids over the contaminated table surface in all directions. They were ready to jump. Like tensed up paratroopers lined up in a plane, as my mind has been made up for ages, since birth actually. Do not change habits and habitats unless you're forced to.

Silence again. A distant call from an owl squeezes through the tilted kitchen window. As if common sense would need any confirmation from outside.

'Expected to do what?' Alan shouts plainly annoyed. 'I have been filling gaps for ages. I'm now replacing this secondary scholar, because bloody Brexit pushed him back from whence he came? I don't know whether you acknowledge the momentum, but an adult sperm whale has just been seen entering British waters near Pevensey. One of the largest marine species of our times and which actually has been flirting with the extinction label for years. It might even be the last living individual ever. And it's struggling. It probably got completely disorientated, most likely intoxicated by poisonous microplastics in our waters that affect its nerve and brain system. A fate much of our marine wildlife is meeting as well. This is an excellent opportunity to monitor chemical poisonings in mammal brains.'

Alan sounds very serious, engaged and pitiful at the same time. I guess I understand his dislike for dishwashing soaps.

'Why don't you use our own brains then?' Aoife jokes.

'Very funny! No seriously! One of the best British whale brain experts is stuck on this bloody hilltop, charting the challenged eel population in the whole of bloody flooded Oxfordshire.'

'Poor chap!' Aoife pats Alan compassionately on the shoulder. 'You looked so excited when you arrived here. Finally a breakthrough in your "academic calvary", Aoife quotes explicitly. 'Shouldering your fishing rods while spilling mud all over the chalet floor because of a knee fall half way up the hill path. We all appreciated your accurate sense of imagery, nailing that dramatic entrance of yours perfectly. We even laughed about it, all together. Quite unique, as we all admit. That's why I remember it so well. Boris even promoted himself the remorseful killer and our gorgeous ginger here claimed Mary Magdalene, of course. Don't you remember, darling?'

Aoife squints at Elizabeth, but she acts as if she's not listening, but as I do recall myself, it was all very Elizabeth like. How she subtly enjoyed imposing herself with a mischievous love life.

The girls look quite pleased with that playful memory. It illustrates their weirdly forged sisterhood, like an alloy of two opposing metals, which origin lies mysteriously enough beyond their own birth. There happens to be a unique picture of their grandmothers in their school years, both visiting Wytham Woods. One in her pyjamas, the other neatly dressed, both facing each other. They are intensely enjoying a shared piece of fruitcake. It is probably taken on an early summer evening in the late sixties. The story goes that Aoife's naughty granny had sneaked out of her Hill End camp bungalow at dusk all by herself and that she had bumped into an outdoor dinner party held by Elizabeth's family in the woods. They had her try all the sweet pies and tarts of the family picnic before they released her. Completely overwhelmed and with a drying polaroid as proof it hadn't been a dream, she returned in that moonlit night back to the crammed bungalow at the other end of the woods. They never met again, but Aoife's granny never forgot the wondrous incident. Aoife heard her granny retelling it on regular demand, whenever the picture on her fridge triggered her curiosity and imagination. She always made it sound like a fairy tale. Aoife kept the discoloured polaroid and took it with her to Wytham. To track the location down. It was a remarkable encounter when she showed it to Elizabeth. The girl in the striped pyjamas, they now joke together, but only after an unhealthy amount of alcohol.

'And we all got into praying for your resurrection,' continues Aoife devoutly, while bringing her hands together. 'And guess what happened after three days? Crammed eel traps!'

Aoife grins. It looks like a triumphant pay back.

'And now there's another cold-blooded creature craving to be skilfully labelled by apparently the one and only living whale brain master on this planet.'

'And stuffed and mounted!' adds Elizabeth suddenly.

'Whales are warm-blooded,' corrects Alan dryly, parrying the pathetic mockery of the girls.

'Why this sudden interest then?'

A clear allegation of Alan's notorious cold-heartedness.

'WE don't keep you here!' David intervenes irritated. He articulates what we're thinking. That we can't decide in Alan's place. We never do, by the way. Each person is responsible for his or her own project, with the excuse not to contaminate its clinical outline and certainly not to steal any personal merits in the likelihood of any academic accomplishment. That's why the flag incident is so extraordinarily sensitive.

'Just go. What keeps you here? Everybody can be missed.' Victimised David clearly aims at his own firing companions who finally deserted. With a bit of persistence, a solitary firing is perfectly feasible, he stubbornly believes. I can see him thinking. Defying his own sad misfortune and fighting the built-up frustrations. There's a thin line between lunacy and passion, they say.

For me they're synonyms. I can tell by the way people look at me. David's cynicism shows that he is feeling exhausted, disappointed, abandoned and probably very, very lonely.

'They will certainly have filled your gap here before you've even sniffed at that rotting carcass,' David continues.

'That counts for whale experts too.' Aoife keeps poking, 'I heard the French are chasing it as well.'

'That's what I was about to say, indeed.' Boris picks in. 'And it is more than interest. They even claim him. It was on my news feed. Just wait a sec.'

Boris digs clearly relieved into his mobile again, that hasn't left the table since dinner, except during David's biological rag attack.

'What if it's a she, by the way.' Aoife corrects for her turn.

'Well, her then. Who cares?'

'I do, with all due respect!' replies Aoife.

'The poor girl must be brain dead then.'

'If not dead, than certainly depressed and suicidal.' Aoife completes. 'Choosing a British pebbled grave! I can't figure out what's worse.'

'Again very funny, girls!' Alan is not amused at all and he doesn't hide it. It's getting serious when subtlety fades.

'If I'm after this dying cachalot, he'll have me stripped alive. If only for breaking a contract.'

'Looks fair to me. Poor eels,' Aoife snarls again.

'I don't kill them. I just chip the adults before they head for the ocean to spawn. This project is my first sincere hope for any serious Oxford perspective. I can't leave, at least not now with these conditions. The flood thrusts the silver ones further inland. I must check the traps daily and some definitely need to be replaced. The current is far too strong, especially when they are full. It's harvesting time, you know. DAMN!'

If he hadn't had his hands in the tub, he would have banged his fist on any hard surface near him. The volume of his voice compensates the missed effect.

'I can't bear the thought of this dying whale being surrendered to the mercy of ratty gulls and ignorant sailing tourists. What should I do?'

'It has to beach first or are they going to chase it, like Moby Dick?' Elizabeth soberly states.

'That's royal fish, is it. I'd inform the Receiver of the Wreck, if I were you.' Aoife backs up Elizabeth, against the bold bastion of boys.

'Too bad her late majesty can no longer benefit from the whalebone shapewear, so there's still hope, Alan.'

Elizabeth winks at Aoife to confirm their camaraderie.

'Here it is!' Boris straightens his back and starts reading.

"FRENCH CLAIM EXTINCT WHALE!"

French fishermen spotted an adult white sperm whale in international waters more than thirty sea miles off the west coast of France. This recently labelled extinct species makes the appearance even more remarkable. It happens to be an isolated female individual. She drew the fishermen's attention by surfacing constantly. The animal was clearly struggling and they alerted the French coastguard for assistance. Soon a boat with two marine biologists was sent from the local sea-centre in Boulogne-Sur-Mer, but when the French experts arrived, the chased whale had already reached British waters. The scientists had to let her go because they lacked permission to track her beyond sovereign borders. They were rather brutally stalled by two British Royal Marine frigates. The incident went all the way up to the French presidential office to get the urgent paperwork in order. The biologists, however, were furious when they realised that the old fish agreements had coincidentally expired and had not been renewed, let alone extended, thanks to the memorable Brexit fishing bills consolidating sovereign fishing grounds. To prevent the animal from further harm the recent coordinates are being kept secret. Rumours have it the animal was last spotted near a less accessible rocky Cornish coastline."

'Ain't this great!' Boris finishes.

'Yeah, fantastic,' echoes Elizabeth ironically while leafing to another page. 'Pevensey in Cornwall, great coverage?'

'Who said Pevensey?' Boris asks.

'I had picked that up somewhere,' Elizabeth remarks sharply from behind her lecture. 'Isn't that where William the Bastard landed before he claimed himself conqueror?

How symbolic. It gives the French intervention a more invasive character, don't you think?'

'It certainly does. And the French only tried to save the poor girl.' Aoife sounds compassionate and theatrical at the same time.

'By pushing her into British waters and the range of vigilant frigates,' Elizabeth adds coldly. 'What a great salvation.'

I want to throw flags into the debate, but relent.

'Have we sent our own marine biologists yet?' Georg questions further.

'Boris reports that they first put all the efforts in keeping the French at bay. Only when the whale has finally beached, they will somehow feel the urge to call some likely royal authorities,' Alan laments.

'Not a daily routine procedure, I presume. *Major, where did we store the latest whale invasion protocol?*' Georg tries a poor imitation of some stereotype ranked officer. The only credibility lies in his forced RP accent.

Nobody laughs.

Alan clearly wants to put an end to all the raillery. For him, there's no reason to keep mocking about. He seems to be the one who is suffering the most. He even carries on milking the doom scenario.

'And what do you get now? All sorts of local, communal, regional and even sectarian stakeholders popping up from nowhere and crawling to this craggy coastline to get their filthy, greedy hands on whatever they think is interesting. Even if it falls under Royal Protection.'

'Are they all crawling to Pevensey?'

'No, of course not. Or perhaps some are, I don't know where that Pevensey rumour comes from. Boris got coordinates from a reliable source, but that was classified info, he said.'

Alan throws an inquisitive, puzzled, and finally irritated look at Boris, but he ignores him completely since he's sucked into new streamings again.

'Classified info, of course.' Elizabeth says understandingly.

'Now calm down, Alan, you don't have to get that upset.' Georg attempts to ease the tension back to normal standards.

'But I do!' Alan protests. 'I feel condemned to these bloody eels. A sperm whale brain isn't available every day. It might be a once in a life time opportunity. Even the last ever. And what keeps me here? Some sexing and chipping for a census to be published in the next year's local eel editorial, which nobody will ever read.'

'Mistake, your tutor will.' Aoife states. 'And he will put you on that chair at the high table you're so desperately after. 'Would they venture eels with greens on the inauguration menu? They surely can miss a couple, won't they, Alan?'

'Why not have some tomorrow? I'd love to try some. You said you catch adult individuals, didn't you?' Georg has now fully re-entered to join the bashing.

'Can you skin them, ladies?'

'I can skin any eel, my boy!' Aoife confesses playfully.

'Why do my eels always lead to sex?' Alan poses.

'Because you're a sublimating pervert, that's what you are. Reading eels, euwgh!' Aoife shivers.

'And sperm whales too, apparently! Yummy!' says Elizabeth.

'Oh, for Christ's sake!' shouts Alan, 'it's not what you think.'

'I don't think whale brains will score any better?' Aoife and Elizabeth keep on teasing.

'Probably not. Although, there are enough nutters in Oxford who would get overexcited by brains bigger than theirs,' Elizabeth completes.

'It's not size that matters, girls,' Boris cunningly interrupts.

'Of course, Boris. You must know for sure.'

'No, seriously.' Georg corrects. 'Boris is right. It has something to do with the consistence of nerve connective tissue within the brain mass. I bet even my dormice can compete with Alan's whale brain.'

'I'm afraid you lost me there.' Elizabeth says. 'Lack of tissue. I surrender.'

Elizabeth chooses a safe withdrawal. Faking stupidity has never harmed anyone. She dives back into her lecture on disruptive effects of psilocybic fungi. I wonder how long she will hold the feigned ignorance. I know she's nailed this skill masterfully, but positioning yourself on the verge of the playing field, keeps you from scoring. I just know, because I never come to really joining a real game.

'So, what are you going to do about it, Alan?'

Aoife confronts him with his own responsibilities. She believes most men get frustrated because they avoid proper action by procrastination and they hope to see others decide in their place. To halve the blame for choosing poorly. What was this whale whining otherwise all about?

But then Boris suddenly intervenes again. 'And... what... if... someone else checked the traps for you?'

Typical of Boris. Sneaky proposals that flirt with pragmatics, ethical objections and common sense.

'Just for a couple of days. Your tutor won't visit us here, I guess. He's desperately lifting his Edwardian furniture in the valley. I mean, counting eels shouldn't be that difficult. One of the ladies seems to have built up enough expertise that they'd be delighted to volunteer for the job, it seems.'

'I beg your pardon?'

Aoife heads for the sink and faces Boris. She's still a bit smaller than he is, but she refuses to get on her toes. She raises her voice to reach that notorious warning level, which usually initiates a Cold War like period lasting between an hour and some days, depending on the matter's nature and the unpredictable twists of any allied forces around.

'Never EVER insinuate what I think or might want to think. Is that clear, mister Boris Shavel?'

I have seen her slapping a boy once and I thought she would do it again, but she doesn't. She must have learnt that violence undermines your position. At least, that's my conviction. She turns her back on Boris without waiting for any response and leaves the room far too theatrically. Elizabeth slams her book at the very same time, jumps up from her hiding spot as if pulled by an invisible thread and joins her sister in arms, demonstratively ignoring everyone else in the room, including me.

I caught a glimpse of Elizabeth's knickers when she lifted her knees to free her feet from under her own weight. It wasn't meant to. It just happened. Accidentally. That's what I try to make myself believe.

'That was perhaps a bit too much, Boris.' Georg breaks the awkward silence again. He sounds assessing.

'Well, she took the cheeky road first, remember.' Alan reacts apologetically.

'Of course she did, Alan.'

'Well, that's my whole point,' says Alan, 'any of my eely entrances gets immediately *phallusised.*'

'I don't think that's an English verb,' David remarks. He usually corrects us, the non-natives, whenever we blunder.

'No, it isn't. And I don't care! It works for her, don't you agree?'

'I guess so, Alan.'

'To *phallusise*! Great! That's our next wiki-item!'

'Not now, Boris,' says Georg.

Boris refers to his obscure hobby of secretly installing fake Wiki-pages. I believe Georg is involved too. They find intellectual pleasure in making up plausible nonsense articles for ingeniously created niches with genuine scientific references, mostly mutually related. It's getting a bit out of hand, in my opinion. I was allowed into their most exclusive club rather by accident. Boris and Georg were plotting on some Brexit related articles, using good old Mr. Lyndon's account and his favourite cat, Arnold, as password, when they suddenly realised I was sharing the same room. I had to take oaths and promise eternal allegiance through solid numbness. Luckily a very convincing trait of mine.

Their phoney feeds look very authentic and therefore hard to uncover, but they undoubtedly lead to dubious myths and conclusions. Their challenge lies in building up credibility, surviving the Wiki-checks and they award each other a bonus for being referred to in other people's entries. Boris's dubious proposal to help out poor Alan in this matter shouldn't surprise anyone within this perspective, but as I've already mentioned, it's getting a bit out of hand.

ACT II

Game

It has been a while since I heard the tawny owls hooting. I guess since the start of the rainfalls, when I picked up poor Margaret's second-hand nail polish lamp in town. Too bad the unnatural weather conditions thwarted its high expectations of diverse and rare finds. I remember it so well because it felt like a curse Margaret had put on her own precious played down gem. The weather has only worsened since I tracked her down behind an innocent looking ad under the category Women's Appliances.

She had looked at me suspiciously, when I handed over the two quid in return. It felt as if she had pushed her only child onto the tattiest school bus, into the hands of an even more dubious tattooed bus driver. She had the lamp all wrapped up in used Christmas paper to prevent it from any more calamities. She had also checked whether I would wipe my feet on her wrung rag that had probably been laid out as a sneaky trap to assess the righteousness of this rare intruder. I even wiped them when I headed back for the door.

'Don't you worry, ma'am. I'll take good care of it!'

But my reassuring words had a reversed effect on her burdened mind. Would the tape hold that kept the plastic switch on its place, since her Rupert had knocked the lamp off the window-sill while taking down the curtains for the yearly spring cleaning? And would I know how to handle the delicate holders when removing the tubes for cleaning? I recognised a distinct hygiene struggle in Margaret's mind-set, which had cancered somewhere in her brain quite nastily. Her back bent downwards to invisible spots on a hideous vintage tablecloth and to the unavoidable dirty tracks on a daily swept kitchen floor. She was slain by the unfair competition of cheaper Eastern European manicurists and an increasingly filthier world. It had given her that unhealthy, grumpy look.

'You're not working for those Polish pimps, are you?'

Margaret's final tick off. She didn't hide her edgy reservations about low cost settled immigrants and clearly angled for pity and sympathy. She displayed herself as being the victim of a lost world she used to brighten up with her own exclusively, probably imported, Polish polish colours. I kept the pun for myself, as usual. She was too upset about her own downfall and the fishy status of the many pop-up massage and beauty shops on the outskirts of town. According to her accounts, they had nicked her clientele without asking. And now they needed an international driving permit themselves to get to Rupert's sister in France. What on earth was going on with her country?

There was a clear shortcut in her reasoning, but I didn't want to throw up politics, mainly because of a looming drizzle. She saw me out, soothed by the idea I seemed more than lawful. I was probably labelled as one of the numerous intensely discussed grown up sons of one of her many lost and forgotten local clients from those long gone, fading days. I didn't look back, avoiding any insinuation of sympathy and understanding. I pushed the pedals brutally downwards, as if held back by a weird wind of concerns and worries.

I left between two showers. My precious purchase uncomfortably squeezed under my armpit while crossing hazardous junctions with one unreliable lousy handbrake. I remember the relief finally riding uphill, pulling the handle bar single-handedly. It pushed me constantly out of balance, all the way up to the old oak, whom I trusted our rusty old trusty bike to. And then I took the last muddy stretch to our cabin in the woods, the chalet. I haven't regretted that bargained treat any second. If only Margaret knew what beauties I have caught so far, despite the awfully wet conditions.

The rainy weather hasn't stopped ever since. The intensity of the flooding surely doubled the weight of every single deed and fact. As if the omnipresence of water has been levelling everything up to new floodline standards.

Due to the forced isolation and strict rationing we share all available resources and energy with the ones we're condemned to work and live with on the hilltop.

Apart from the rats, badgers and voles, I consider the others being sentenced to a much heavier confinement with me than I'm with them. The bungalow has its limits, but not our private oddities, I'm afraid.

The girls are brilliant, in a way. Not just joyful, but even noticeably attractive, which is always comforting if you're driven to daily conciliations. I prefer Elizabeth, the ginger one. Noble Kentish roots, they say, with links to pre-royal Tudor times. She's probably named after the late queen. Poor soul, then, I think. Always being hooked to this much cherished British benchmark and is therefore probably more fictitiously nudged than the daily newsfeeds. That looming threat of ever-present aristocratic expectancies in dark mirrored corners, to perform at least as well as honourable standards tell, whatever that might mean. I see her suffer, from time to time, waging an internal war on her own beautiful bodily battlefield, leaving blushes, frowns and scars. Whatever traditional pedigree is pulling at her, the sharp edges of her born existence cut more deeply into her soul than the exquisite short dissection blade her father gave her before she was dropped off at Lincoln College with the unspoken message to deliver, again, like everybody else had done beyond the beginning of her dusty family chronicles. It felt like giving an ashtray to a tobacco addict. This was her family's cynical way of dealing with self-mutilation. Poor Elizabeth, I think again. If the flag thief only knew. I know because I'm a silent observer. I look when people don't expect I'm looking. Like watching with a white stick and sunglasses. I just don't need the accessories. I blend into the wall, like a sleeping night moth.

It's more than preference, frankly. Not particularly due to my fondness of mushrooms, or perhaps a little, but I like Elizabeth a lot. She has nothing posh or elitist about her. She's just her own vulnerably beautiful self. And her nimble mind makes me dance on hot coal-. She makes me stumble and generous at the same time. And that is weird, considering I've always been a lad on my own, with his odd rules and tricks and ticks between him and the rest of the universe.

Elizabeth is a mycologist. She strives to the very marrow of her bones to meticulously categorise mushrooms and fungi in the woods. The wet weather has made them thrive as never before and that's how she got hooked up with us. She realised she couldn't return to the hill once they were about to block the river road to Wytham at what doubtfully looked like low tide. I watched her crossing the strip anyway, against all advice and common sense, barefoot, with water washing up to her knees, muscled snow white thighs steadily supporting her and walking boots dangling over her shoulders. She argued she couldn't live with the idea of waiting for lower river levels behind her squared college room window while an overload of boleti was flourishing and screaming for scientific attention on these lush hillsides. We all benefit from her findings as she safely delivers the edible and smokeable species, nicely cut after being photographed, counted and catalogued. The rare gems get dried and stored in obscure wooden cabinets in the biology department room, which she automatically promoted to her personal bedroom too.

Actually, everybody has claimed a room in the chalet to secure that much appreciated privacy considering the extended confinement till further notice, including me. The chalet has turned into some sort of Scandinavian Hogwarts, inspired by IKEA's notorious soulless fantasy policy. The square shaped staircase is perhaps the only provoking feature in the bleak central hall, linking all the "houses" like one solid wooden spine with the kitchen and the necessary exit into the woods. The nutty kids are obvious and the departments aren't the best of friends, like always. They hardly cooperate unless personal interest is involved. And yes, even witchcraft seems sometimes scaringly present. The only difference might be the obscure passageway into this other world. No simple platform, rabbit hole or wardrobe, but a complicated puzzling algorithm triggered from the first intellectual spark in the cradle.

Even in this time of drownings some things do prosper surprisingly and profit lavishly from the abundance of water and the world's distraction to less trivial things like soaked stalled rubbish.

There is water all over, which doesn't bother me a lot frankly. On the contrary, I must confess. A reversed Brexit and an alternative lockdown, I call it. An island within an island. Forcing rats, badgers, deer and some quirky people upwards, to Wytham Hill. Cut off from town and gown by an untameable River Isis, being happily neglected by the rest of the world because of much greater concerns over insurance claims.

I drop my pen, which rolls to the middle of my opened moth book. David left some minutes after the girls' exit, back to his raging monster who keeps wailing for wood like a hungry baby for milk. He's off for the final night. The climb to the 1,200 °C glazing summit, with a new supply of coffee and biscuits from his own personal reserve. Boris, Georg and Alan cleared the kitchen much later in some weird sort of suspicious plotting togetherness. It revived my expectancy of the girls to return, but all in vain. I realise I can't keep recounting my data in the hope that Elizabeth would rejoin me in the kitchen. If only for a quick sip from the fridge. The intervals of the owls are extending. I must move myself before it gets really awkward.

I give up the daydreams and get myself to the back room to dig up my old scuffed wellies from behind a robust plastic potato chest. I'm about to venture out into the soggy darkness while listening to the starving owls nearby. They loathe rain, just as I do, for the pouring corrupts any accurate hunting skill. I hear rats running off while I reach for my adequate footgear. Our source of starch is getting more vital every day. If we hadn't had the solid plastic container, the rodents and badgers surely would have gone after it. That would mean disaster since the situation has turned us into surrendered vegetarians. We have run short of bread and nuts, as the former has moulded and most of the latter is labelled unsuitable for human consumption. Especially the badgers have become more bold and brutal. You hear them scratching and munching on whatever we've left them. Boris says it is our duty to help them out in these challenging times, but I'm more and more convinced that Boris, and Georg as well, are too lazy to walk all the way to the green container and that they happily take any excuse to show it.

Wytham's official badger patrol disembarked the woodland project when the first floodings were reported. They were confident the animals wouldn't be affected by the water. They thought themselves of their own situation otherwise, so they left. The badgers must have realised by now that the massive amount of cages piled up next to the chalet was nothing but an idle threat. Ivy has regrown into them and it would take weekends to make them useful again. The determined badgers visit us every night. I hope we run out of food long before the patrol returns, but I fear the badgers won't have enough time to unlearn this unnatural feeding routine. They look too smart to me. Perhaps they eat human flesh as well. Only then our lazy reputation might be saved.

Five days rations are left, hereby skipping vegan Aoife who banned animal related ingredients since she definitely left her United States more than a year ago. Weirdly enough, she ignores the laboratorial dietary nut prescriptions on the labels by allowing the lidded bowls plainly in our communal dining area. Aoife quickly shifts into this survival mode. It's like a second nature, as if she's raised as such. And there is more to it than just environment and conservation. The fanatic way in which she positions herself in social debates, her notorious staggering and the accompanying hard-boiled arguments only prove for me some genuine personal injustice in her lifetime.

They know I'm out by now. They are used to hearing me wandering about just after sunset to light the moth traps all over the terrain. The dry intermissions have become so scarce that the routine feels somehow awkward and that my expectancy has faded to a more realistic, read common, outcome.

My eyes need time to adjust to the darkness. I don't want to slip on some wet roots and end up face down in the soggy soil. I hope to keep my hands clean and dry. My precious loot won't allow sticky fingers. Once cold and wet, it always takes ages to get the hands acclimatised again.

'Be careful, the owls are out.'

Aoife shouts from an open skylight above my head.

'And the bats! And the wolves!'

I squeak too loud for my nature in order to stop the conversation right there and I howl from behind my flappy rain cap. I want to sound funny to mask the abrupt blocking, but I feel I don't really succeed. I speed up my pace although the path curves slightly uphill. I know Aoife doesn't deserve this. She's the only one left who hasn't really given up talking to me freely, despite my numerous hilarious escape routes.

'How can I finish your Wodehouse copy if I have to turn off lights before bedtime? I feel like a punished girl.'

'I bet you deserve it!' I shout back.

Her lights are out indeed. They know by now, that when my lighting time is nigh, they must switch off theirs. Some just close shutters or roll down curtains. It all happens nearly automatically.

My instructive requests must have impressed, since they've been loyally obedient, apart from some isolated cases of nightly stupor. Concerns about my project render me talkative, usually in front of the coffee machine. I mark clear mental mine fields. I set out safe borders others should not cross and I do this with the help of the soothing fragrance of coffee. It turns opponents cooperative, approachable, or at least immobile for a predictable notice of time.

Our projects grow strangely enough into certain parallelisms. Again we resemble a wide phalanx of weirdly disciplined individuals, making up a secret division in Her Majesty's Service to protect and maintain the all too Common Natural Wealth. Within this perspective, the flag incident should be taken very seriously. Sabotage is considered treason in military ranks, isn't it? We should have the bastard skinned, spiked, and finally cut to munchable pieces for the badgers, shouldn't we? I'm sometimes scared of my own medieval outbreaks. It reminds me of Margaret's hardboiled mindset, as if facing bigger enemies wipe out centuries of rationalism.

I always feel the others spying from behind their darkened windows, me regularly checking the invisible barbed wire that keeps them compliant. Like anthropologists, they observe that weird lonely nocturnal delta male private, who bends over some poorly installed egg cartons overnight and who brings them excitedly within the premises when the sun is up. It turns me into a scrutinised object myself. Not really having figured out whether I would want to be touched by their wet and sticky fingers. Elizabeth's nails mostly show traces of brownish dirt.

I see Aoife's cigarette firing up as she sucks some air through it. I still can't see how she squares that circle. She's the only smoking vegan I know on my planet. I think she converted after she got addicted. Living with that paradox must turn people crazy. She would stand my hill test, for sure.

I take the short cut to My Lady's Seat, heading to The Singing Way. The humming way would be more appropriate for me, but at least its embracing brings comfort and makes me sing inside. That's what walking does to me. It automatically paces a welling melody, mostly with a repetitive character. I toy with tiny variations along the way. And when I'm really in a good mood, I might recite Tolkien. Over and over again, because roads go ever ever on, don't they?

I've installed five light traps in the various habitats Wytham Woods have to offer in order to harvest as many different species as possible. They're mostly a bit hidden from walkers' view. Margaret's wonder lamp is on The Great Ash summit, the last stop on my round, as if to keep the best for last.

The moon lights the track between the spells of rain and casts quirky shadows on the dark terrain. I refuse to use a torch. It blinds more than you think, as paradoxical as that may sound. I even avert my gaze when I switch on a battery or generator. Or I close one eye, to protect my acquired night vision. I try to develop other senses too. When one sticks daily to the same route, the brain automatically maps trees, puddles, and roots along the track with obstacles and points of interest. You build up an emotional memory a scientist should probably avoid. But how to resist the repetitive glancing at branches where short-eared owls normally roost or the hesitation before cornering to anticipate surprised foxes or badgers on the many hollow roads? Not to mention the mechanisms I stick to, which I believe guarantee more success since they have accidentally proven so. My lighting routine has gradually evolved into a complex mixture of habits, calculated actions, and fragile superstitions. Every round confirms and adjusts details at the same time, like a new layer of paint covering or redefining lines and colours. Frankly, there's no great science that justifies my handlings. My own built up complexity just gives me the acquired comfort and soothes my ever raging nerves.

The first moth trap lies just behind the first hill range. My grandfather would say "on the military line". He was sent to the Falklands when my dad was little. He brought my father back a souvenir: this wooden display of the Queen of Falklands Fritillary, their local, most famous butterfly, pinned on a cream white linen cushion. For my father it was a clear token that his dad had returned sick of warfare, but when I was little myself, I couldn't perceive any peaceful signals in the spiked butterfly. It obtained a sanctified status when granddad died of covid a couple of years ago. That mysterious mantelpiece object once triggered me into the world of the lepidoptera, which isn't that peaceful either, I'm afraid. To me the aggression lies mainly in their numerous predators and threats. From birds and parasites to climate change and industrialised agriculture.

My last biology teacher in secondary school once advised me to choose my object wisely when he heard I would adventure a PhD in Biology. "One tends to gradually alter into the scrutinised creature," he said, and I think he was right. Sometimes I feel myself the Gregor Samsa of the hilltop, a name I gave myself on Instagram, a poor attempt of bonding with so called moth mates.

'Not all those who wander are lost.'

Elizabeth! I recognise her voice out of a million. I petrify inside. An adapted form of thanatosis. She, here, now! I imagine a billion other insects crawling into a better position to watch me freeze. I can't hide since I've left my pupal phase of the day. Would she have waited till this next vulnerable stage to get after me? My flashy raincoat makes camouflage attempts hilarious.

'I said not all those who wander are lost.'

The trick is to endure as long as needed. Until they lose interest. It worked many times. But this is Elizabeth, the bright white-legged Elizabeth, whose knickers disrupted my mental archive like an aggressive pheromone. She is at the same time the only accredited hilltop person to dismantle my multi-layered protective instinct. I feel trapped, like my poor devils at dusk, caught in the most blinding setting they had ever dreamt of. What is she after? And why? Convincing me with an abused Tolkien verse. Does it reveal her true and fair nature as well? As if she claims some royal ancestry? Perhaps she does.

'I didn't know you were a Tolkien fan.'

A pupal sound leaves my body. Uncontrollably. Taking over and giving in to the dark irresistible stimuli from within, like the last autumnal monarch butterfly mysteriously heads south again, driven by an inexplicable force as if it had caught instructive secrets in the cooling breezes. Just let go, Bernie! Follow the bright-legged light. Even if you end up spiked and framed on her mantelpiece.

'Who isn't?' I say.

She jumps from a giant pile of timbered logs. It looks like she has been waiting for me. Her white legs have turned blueish black. I go for the skinny jeans, but it's far too dark to let my eyes wander.

'I thought I needed a bit of fresh air to get both feet back on the ground.'

Her boots land in a puddle and splash mud all over. Probably up to my trousers but I don't care.

'Do you mind if I walk along?'

She ignores my doubts and fears and just gets next to me, treading my nocturnal Humming Way. She shares my pace and, why not, along with the thundering secret melodies in my head, heading into a darkening world I'm about to light.

'I've always been curious about your nightly walks? Surely you don't mind?'

'No, not at all.' I can't figure out whether I'm lying or not. My head is raging with opposing alarm checks.

'Is it OK if I talk? I always get scared in the dark and by talking I hope to ban all those terrifying sounds. Your moths don't have ears, do they? I mean, they're not scared off by noise, are they?'

'No, of course not.'

How could they? Her voice is like sweet strokes. I think along, as she walks beside me, and I'm happy with her eruptive nature, as she tries to calm down her own spooky demons in her own funny way.

Two rolling fireball marbles along the Wytham track. I'm afraid we might bounce off when we hit.

'I must give in, I sneaked out and waited for you here because I don't want the others to know. It would only lead to tiring misunderstandings.'

'No problem. I understand,' I say. I'm a professional at understanding misunderstandings, I complete for myself.

'I had nearly given up and considered going back. It's getting pretty dark now. Aren't you later than usual?'

It would sound bizarre if I confessed I had been waiting for her in the kitchen. It's an ironic world. Nature surprises you with accidental encounters in the least expected moments, while you have been chasing them zealously before.

'Nights remind me too much of home, you know.'

I just let her talk and listen. It calms me down in a certain way, the pace of our steps and her nervous little sounds.

She continues, 'I used to sleep in the attic of our old family manor. My dad had convinced me in bright daylight. I was taken by the round windows giving way to the meadows and the walled rose gardens and their framed shadows on the opposing leaning walls. But the nights were horrible. I heard rodents running all over. Gale winds would make the beams creak and in the summer the bats would flutter in and out of every cranny of the top floors. I really hated the place at night. And I still do, actually. I refuse to sleep in my old bed when I come over. I always tell my parents it's too far from the heated toilet. That's sincerely true, but there's more, of course, which I keep for myself. They would only try to talk it out of me. They always do. I prefer the smallest guest room, just above the kitchen. Cynthia's homely noises comfort me, at dusk and dawn. And the smell of fresh bread and coffee in the morning is priceless. Don't you miss home sometimes?'

We arrive at the first trap, which allows me to ignore her invasive question. She lights her torch without warning and blinds my bearings. She should understand her question was not very appropriate.

'Do you need any help?'

She comes closer and even kneels down too. I sense a genuine commitment to assist me in whatever lies ahead. I'm not used to this kind of intimate collaboration. I rely on routine while my brains freak out, but I can't be angry with Elizabeth. I really can't.

'Do instruct me if I can be of any help,' she insists.

I get some weird but distinct sharp fragrance in exchange for a ruined night vision. The beam finally lands on the right spot and I start to lift the plastic litter bag that functions as a rain cover.

'Shall I fold this up for you?'

She pulls the plastic out of my hands and hands me the torch.

'Here, take this. I have no clue where to aim at. You're the professional after all.'

Indeed I am, or at least I should be, but I panic even more and tremble for my handlings are being brutally disrupted. The torch light lands on her knees as she stretches them to let the bag hang down to drain. A slight breeze pushes the plastic against her legs, which makes her pivot instantly.

'Oh my God, I'm so hopeless.'

'You're doing fine.' And we both laugh at our own shameful performances.

She copies my unique folding routine. It makes me genuinely happy and to my surprise I giggle out loud. The beam flashes all over as I wrest the folded bag out of her hands and shove it swiftly under the right lamp leg on the side of the switches.

'I don't know how you manage this all by yourself.'

'And in complete darkness!' I add. I don't know why I say this, but it feels like all the justified messages are being crammed in. Distilled from a boiling mind. I quickly switch on the black light and my nerves get completely overrun by the bright, bluish rays.

'Wow!'

Elizabeth is clearly overwhelmed by the contrast. And I am too, to be honest. A sudden shock neutralises the moment. A mental blast followed by a sweet high-pitched whistle.

Her torchlight looks even more ridiculous now.

'I didn't know it was that bright.'

'I've many sorts. This one is pretty moderate. Only 630 lumen. It's the lack of light around us that enhances the effect.'

'If they love the light so much, why don't they fly in bright daylight? Are they too ugly for sunlight?'

'Good question. It's not because we label them as night moths that we should consider them ugly,' I answer. 'They avoid most predators, apart from bats. That's how they've evolved. Let's say they appreciate the slightest lighting even more, because they lack it.'

'Like minors and alcohol on Minorca.'

'I guess so.'

'There are extremely beautiful species all around, even in the UK. There's now the annual University Moth Challenge. And I am participating again.'

'And are you successful?'

'Top ten.'

'That's not bad.'

'I don't know. It just is.'

'You're far too modest. There's something about you. Some hidden brightness. I guess you're just like your moths. They pretend death, but when you don't look they fly up. I like that. You just don't show it.'

'That's called thanatosis. A brilliant trick. And why should I?'

There is a short silence. I don't know how to react. It seems that Elizabeth fancies me. That's all I can think of.

'You're the luring lantern lighter then.'

Elizabeth sounds suddenly excited. She even repeats her alliterating finding. 'The luring lantern lighter!'

I'm quite happy with the epitheton. I had much worse in my school days. It sounds witty and kind. And sexy. Would this luring relate to the lantern or to the lighter himself? Typical Elizabeth.

'I don't actually hunt or kill them,' I respond. 'Most of them survive my humble interference. It's a bit like Alan's eels. I just count and observe my catch in the morning and then I release them.'

'By deceiving them with light.'

'They love it. I actually give them a good time. The light energy calms them down.'

The image of the luring lighter sharpens.

'A bit like television and smartphones.'

'If you say so.'

I openly confess the deceiving features in my proceedings and I wonder at the same time whether they would be happier without my interventions?

'You turn them into addictive empty-headed little devils, if you ask me,' Elizabeth teases. Always a bit critical, but in a healthy way. Usually to tone down overgrown issues.

'They just follow their nature,' I parry.

'I think we all do, don't we? Some more than others, I guess. I think it can get quite complicated, wearing, and time consuming to get a notion of one's own nature. Certainly when you feel you need to seek in less common or convenient directions. Because once you even consider unconventional paths, it's so hard to convince others they might lead to similar sunny valleys as well. I myself am still wandering, if you understand what I mean?'

In the silence that follows, I see Elizabeth battling and groping behind the blind spots generated by the luring lamp.

'You know,' Elizabeth tries again, balancing her words and body in her own crazy darkness, 'I don't know how to say this, but... when Aoife is around, she always gets me so...'

She suddenly stumbles and grabs my arm for support.

I react instantly, ignited as it were, by the sudden physical contact.

'I know exactly what you mean. I think we're so conscious about ourselves that we've gradually been making up our own favourable nature. And yes, why not take Aoife as a silly example. Are we really carnivorous or did we turn into meat lovers because the supply was more abundant and fresh all year round? Some luscious species might have crossed our tracks accidentally, or even better, were so willing to mate in our stinking, feeding presence that they agreed blindly to the appalling contract that allowed us to slaughter their offspring in return for food and conditioned safety. Is Aoife therefore right by sticking to that vegan diet or is she actually ignoring her true call of nature? I can't really figure that out. We just think too much, don't you think? Well, there you have it. Thoughts again. They drift us too far away from who we really are or who we were meant to be. If there is any purpose anyway, as most biologists are convinced there is no goal in evolution at all. I think that's the problem, we create our own wickedly calculated causes and goals. Probably including my nightly moth tracking and Alan's sudden eel interest. Why do we keep doing the unnatural things we do?'

I have no idea where these words come from. They're not new, at least not the thoughts, but what on earth brought me to this chaotic eruption? The only reasonable explanation I have, is that Elizabeth is listening. And nobody else but she. Apart from some billion bugs and beetles and a puzzled fox perhaps.

She seems silenced by my words or at least by their impulsive character. I doubt whether I should have spoken, because my thoughts are not really comforting her. On the contrary.

I'm tempted to consider myself a blithering idiot. I fear I have numbed her like an ignorant talkative school teacher on a first school day. Why am I so hopeless at nightly conversations with a girl I fancy, in the middle of a lonesome wood? The darkness is pushing us forward, from one frightful silence to the next. The owls are doing their best in breaking them.

At last, Elizabeth suddenly starts talking again. She has changed the subject, fortunately.

'I think they're fooling Alan.'

'Who is?' I say nearly automatically and relieved.

Elizabeth brings the conversation back to a tangible level. She must have interpreted my philosophical nonsense in her own pragmatic way, which is perfectly reasonable. Even favourable and recommendable. A healthy counter-balance, if you like. Why not even complementary? But that's my cautious wishful thinking. Thinking again.

We start heading northeast now, towards David's kiln site. Elizabeth is still walking next to me. The canopy opens up and the road becomes more inviting, gradually, the closer we get to the fields. She releases my arm. I think in fear of being caught.

'Boris. And probably Georg too.'

'What makes you think so?'

'This whole whale story. A Cornish Pevensey? Come on! A painful slip-up, if you ask me. They've done many similar things in the past. At least Boris has and Georg slavishly follows for any guaranteed amusement.'

'I don't see the fun, actually.'

'You're an exception, Bernie. And please, take that as a compliment.'

'Do you think they have been fiddling with your flags too?'

'I don't know. You're innocent unless you've been proven otherwise, aren't you? But I have my suspects.'

'Am I a suspect?'

'Don't be ridiculous.'

I feel an instant relief. Elizabeth is confiding. To me. I get exclusive information, an indirect confirmation she doesn't dislike me. On the contrary, I'm promoted to a sort of trusted therapist. An allied friend to talk to.

'And if you were, I wouldn't tell you, would I?' she adds rather soberly.

'And what about Aoife?' I tease alternately.

'What about her?'

'Do you suspect her as well?'

'What makes you think that?' Elizabeth stops and pulls my arm to do the same. The beam lights my face deliberately. It looks like I'm being questioned. There's a hostile tone in her voice. I close my eyes to secure my night vision, but in vain. I'm too late. Yellow-green spots flicker behind my closed lids.

'I don't know,' I parry instinctively. 'Just silly guesswork, as well. I'm sorry. Please, calm down!'

My panic has its impact. The torch is lowered and the grip on my arm loosens.

'Then leave the guesswork to me, all right Bernie,' says Elizabeth soothingly.

'It's my project and my problem. I shall deal with this juvenile nonsense myself.'

The spots flash before my feet, but they seem to fade the more I blink. I trust my memory and resume my walking.

'By the way, it is not as serious as you might think. I only make it bigger to demonise the culprit even more, that's all.'

Elizabeth has calmed down. She's talking normally again.

'So you're convinced it's a man?' I try.

'There are not many options left, are there? I don't see badgers replanting little flag poles neatly across discarded sanitary towels in the many fairy rings in the forest?'

Would she be testing me? Confronting her next possible suspect with embarrassing details? Eyeball movement analyses are useless while fighting a lost night vision. Why suggesting a VD infection anyway?

I fall silent. Immediately. I freak. I don't want to ruin things again. I panic. I cannot do anything except insist on resuming our walk, with a gentle mental draw to finish the lighting business. And I think. And rethink. All options are instantly decimated by the ambiguous game she might be playing on me. I'm completely lost, although I bloody well realise where I am.

We both don't say a single word while leaving the Humming Way. The marbles have clearly hit.

I think of the numbing way. A stupid pun, but it holds my mental horses. Where did it derail? What did we talk about before we deviated? Of course. Alan's mammal. How could we have lost it?

'Why would they do this?' I finally resume. 'I mean making up this whale story?'

'I don't know? To tease Alan, for sure. Because they're bored? Because they can? There's something about it. The story has the right balance between detail and vagueness. And it has the required weight as well. An amount of significance and urgency at the same time. An extinct whale popping up again, somewhere near, but we don't exactly know where.'

She puts some magic in her intonation to enhance the mystery effect.

'It's a perfect tease, if you ask me. If you just imagine Alan's life. Little Alan has always been fascinated by whales since primary school. Being born in Switzerland has only catalysed the boy's dream. His granny knits him whale jumpers for Christmas every year. He plunders the whole whale shelf in his local libraries. His dad shows him the whopper in London and buys him a skeleton model building kit which ends up on his desk, dragging him all the way through his horrid, boring secondary schooling. When he's eighteen he flies to the Hebrides, on his own, to catch a glimpse of any of these mammals, but no fin is spotted. His imagination and frustration grow. And when he finally completes his biology studies at university, he nails his PhD on preserved whale brains in the vain hope of a close encounter on any of those long-awaited funded science trips. And then he painfully faces the appalling verdict of extinction. Unfortunate Alan exchanges his fairy creatures with slimy eels to save his academic dream. I think he has the longest career of us all. He's in his mid-thirties, did you know that?'

I wonder what she thinks about my case. Would she have a similar elaborated narrative ready? And would she share it with the others as well?

'How do you know all this?' I ask her instead.

'Guesswork again, but it's too obvious for me, you see. The way it upsets Alan. They enjoy it. Why would they keep bringing it up all the time? And they have the means. You remember that hoax about that so called moon tree in Wytham Woods? Some seeds that had been on Apollo 14 to the Moon? Fifteen of those germinated seeds ended somewhere in the UK. Boris made half of England believe it was one of the many solitary Douglas fir trees near the north facing slope on Wytham Hill. Without any scientific evidence. Aoife said he had once confessed this to her in one of his rare courtship moods. Even if he had been bragging about it, it still proves his mischievous mindset. The article this whole tree hype originated from, was probably published in some well-chosen nooks of the web. Like a parasite it had been waiting to be picked up by some scoop addicted journalist and the ball got rolling. The news reached the university authorities from a different angle of course. They were completely overwhelmed by the sudden massive interest. Didn't you catch any bits of the buzzing?'

'I can't remember, to be honest.'

I answer embarrassed. I sound ridiculous, but she doesn't notice. The question was rhetorical, apparently. She's completely into the story and carries on without an actual pause. We're passing a badgers' sett and a popular observation spot, but I decline to mention any of it in fear of bringing up sensitive associations or whatever. I'm happy she's blathering again.

'Because no one could really confirm nor refute the fact, it lived its own life. And it thrived. Boris had also put up wild cameras to tot up so called believers. He even showed poor Aoife footage of a nocturnal moon shag. Spaffing under the moon tree, he called it. It was brilliant and he was overly excited! It rendered that extra weight to his immortal credibility amongst his wealthy soulmates, I guess. Even today people from all over the world still sneak by to collect cones, seeds, and bark from the supposed site. Coordinates and pictures got so eagerly spread and shared that the university decided not to fight the myth any longer. Never poke a dying fire, they thought, but it didn't die. It kept finding fuel and creeping along, at a steady pace. Fuming. Mystifying.

You know, once an idea is thought, it is impossible to unthink it, don't you think? And when you broadcast that idea, it's even worse. It nestles itself in your brain, like a malignant metaphor framing your reasoning. It's like watching a documentary on ants and feeling itches all over for days. You plant a silly story seed and it automatically germinates by those who want to read or hear it. It always sticks to the same pattern. It's only a matter of time to make it heard, to have it picked up by some ignorant devil. Like an aggressive weed.

'It seems we are oh so easily deceived,' I finally conclude.

'Yes, I think we are,' Elizabeth smiles, 'like your tiny sneaky moths.'

ACT III

Fire

'Still one to go.'

It's remarkable how easily Elizabeth fits into my complex lighting procedures. And I too generate a flexibility I never could imagine. I feel sedated by her presence, giving in to unforeseen alternatives. My proceedings look different, even though the predictable character of my tour tries to tell me otherwise.

I sense dynamics. I interact. Without a single word or reason. I just anticipate. The mechanism lies in our mutual handlings. One igniting the other as it were.

The sharp smell of stoked wood prickles my nose. We're getting close to David's kiln site on the other end of the meadow, but some upcoming haze blocks any clear sight. A yellowish light strangely rims the grey damp trails of a moist forest night breeze coming from under the canopy. Mist is gathering across the open grass area.

'Do you have a similar analysis of Boris?'

Not that I'm not eager to hear Elizabeth's version of my own past, but I don't have the courage to ask her and I probably lack the inevitable exciting plot twisting ingredients as well.

'Of course I have. But I don't think our walk will be long enough,' she replies.

'Just the highlights then.'

'They're only but highlights, I'm afraid. Depending on the observer's perspective, of course, but I might try to end with a climax.'

'Or a happy ending.'

'You're naughtier than I thought, lonely rider.'

'What do you mean?'

'Never been into massages, have you?'

'Not really, no. Why?'

'Never mind. You will come across some hopefully. I sincerely wish you plenty.'

Elizabeth gives me this most generous glance. I get completely overwhelmed and feel my heart being gently pierced onto a silky soft cushion, but then she alters tone, teasingly, and starts a new narrative.

'Boris is an invention of his own imagination. Do you know why he's reading history?' she intones rhetorically, again. 'Because this nation is so much cast in its own ponderous concrete past that every hint of change or progress struggles with laming waves of anxieties. It tries eagerly to consolidate what has always been and it wants us to believe that the old hierarchy and politics are still relevant. It has turned us into tourists in our own country, only allowed to look at our national treasures from a safe distance, nicely kept from the daily trimmed grass. You know why there is a great barrier built around HP? To prevent people from pinching crumbling sandstone into their pockets. The building is falling apart. Most windows can't be opened or they exchanged their insulating capacities for inconvenient draughts, and people get paid to patrol 24/7 to watch over possible short circuit fire hazards in the basements. It's symbolic for our democracy. They try to dig up and polish the old grandeur and they used the Brexit saga as a pep talk. They want to keep up the dying spirit at all costs, but, to me, the sick whale has already beached and some very nasty creatures benefit from its stiffened immobility. The whale-fall has long started.'

It might be a coincidence but the whale image surfaces again, like some sort of archetypal metaphor. It's weird to hear the whole political constitution being bluntly pilloried by Elizabeth. She is poking aggressively into the rotting roots from which she had unwillingly emerged herself, I guess.

'History is one of the most fictitious niches in the wide range of sciences, don't you think?' Elizabeth continues.

'Isn't that a rather narrow reading of the subject?' I try.

'FORTIS EST VERITAS captures it all, doesn't it?' she answers. 'It's the department's invincible ironic credo. Historians have invented the concept truth to serve power and the attempt to keep up with it. And they even made a science out of it. I know what I'm talking about. This country has been going down for decades and nobody seems to notice, because old-school institutions blind us with pomp and circumstance. My father read history as well, but being a Lord in the House hasn't given him one single second of courage to question his lousy democratic position and his whole bloody masquerade. He has been acting solely in the interest of self-preservation.'

Elizabeth is nearly marching. She's taking sturdy steps, as if she tries to synchronise with her thoughts. I cannot judge her insinuations correctly, that the good old imperial spirit has lost all sense of direction and purpose and that politics clearly show superiority withdrawal symptoms. It all makes sense, but I feel myself a lost tourist, completely relying on his talkative guide.

'Perhaps I have been working on mushrooms too long, but dead material is big business. You cannot imagine the numerous sneaky recycling strategies of Nature. And I don't see why it should be different for British nobilities and their valets. Bond is another striking example. He's one big hollow branding attempt to polish our failing standards. And it works. The whole planet believes we have the means and intelligence to produce righteous gentlemen, but we only deliver creatures like Boris. Why else does everyone want to have their children educated here?'

There is a brief interval. A short-circuit. A spark between two bouncing marbles.

'I'm sorry, Bernie. I don't blame you for being here. And I certainly don't mean I don't want you here. You're deceived as well. That's all I'm saying. You just cannot imagine how much I hate this island.'

Elizabeth's rage has suddenly disappeared. As if a shameful reflection has pulled her back into the reserved posture she was cast in. I don't know what to say or do. I liked her streaming voice. Even if it was more like draining. I need to say at least something. To make her believe I don't feel offended or targeted at all.

'I believe historians are for some reason crucial. To bring order in that chaos. To tell truth from fake. To set things right. And yes, there are devilish excesses in every branch. You do know Nobel's legacy.'

'That's not what I'm saying.' She sounds different now. More forgiving, embracing, understanding. 'Of course you're right, but even then, there is a lot of guesswork involved. People like Boris fill up holes. They link dead ends, literally and metaphorically. He has the means and tricks. He knows how to bring the meekest things to life and he uses his know-how to master the present and future as well. As a true Etonian, he got his training right. He's the very product of his own education.'

'Aren't we all?'

'Not in such a way that one has institutionalised his own successful outcome. Schools like Eton don't pay taxes, did you know that? How else can you explain their arrogance towards ordinary life. It's all a matter of consolidating their own success. A perpetual preparedness to avoid a deplorable death. The brutal fear of a lousy legacy.'

Says the person with the longest pedigree of the hill. Perhaps that's why she can put things into perspective.

She's been there. She must have been weighed down by the disastrous impact of tradition and the fictitious backwash of time. And who am I, a lowlandish marsh character, to argue that?

'Is he from Eton?' I pose prudently. 'I thought he had Polish roots.'

'He has,' Elizabeth answers, 'but that doesn't exclude the gateway to a British elitist education, does it? I always had numerous non-natives in class at boarding school. Anyway, he ticks off all the features. The awful regard for birth and position. The knowledge of Aoife descending from an Irish navvy rendered him deferential, not to mention contemptuous.'

'He is spoilt like hell,' Elizabeth continues. 'Always showing off with the latest gadgets. And then his global network of so-called civilised friends. His ubiquitous arrogance, having been everywhere, whenever an earthy spot is mentioned. With all respect, Bernie, he's even been to your place. And worst of all, it is usually attached to some unique sounding experience no one else can overbid. He's addicted to superiority. A die-hard narcissist. And when he smells defeat, he will do whatever he can to regain position. Even by faking. The Etonian way, you see.'

Elizabeth's portrait of Boris turns out quite brutal. Inspired by an obscure modernist painter addicted to psychedelic mushrooms, if you ask me. Daring, aggressive and experimental. Too rude to my opinion and crammed with dubious prejudices, which even he doesn't deserve, I guess. Perhaps understandable, but I doubt countable.

Elizabeth has even raised her voice again. I wonder whether tomorrow's outcome will differ from my standard findings, supposedly night moths do have ears.

'Rumours have it he tracked Roman's lost Ninth Legion back down to his uncle's massive estate in Cumbria, a couple of miles south of Carlisle. He seemed to have found old snippets of Roman tiles on this massive stretch of land. One suggesting a lousy right end of a V followed by four distinct vertical carvings. The clay artefact is too worn for a conclusive determination and the site too expansive to gather coherent details and too remote to make access evident, but exclusive enough to trigger significant interest. Another whale story, if you ask me.'

'Be careful where you tread.'

We now pass a very rooted part, which I mostly take cautiously, with bare hands foolishly stretched before me, anticipating any nasty head-first fall forward, but Elizabeth soldiers on, like a trained military with a mission, target fixed and well-picked weaponry to her disposal. It's obvious Boris has to be put down, no matter how. I try to think along with her, keeping up her pace, finding a way to justify her brutality, but the roots freak me out and she's already too far ahead for me to get hold of any arm or shoulder. Calling her back would only make me look more gawky and hopeless.

The glow from David's firing becomes very visible now. I can even see his posture reflecting whenever he opens the feeding hole to throw some wood in.

'LOOK! David's not alone.'

Elizabeth stalls. She stretches her arm and waits for me to catch up.

'Who the hell is with him? And she has her top off?'

Frontal nudity has always affected me some way or another. Female fronts obviously the most, but I must confess men's torsos too, more precisely the massively worked out muscles I can hardly imagine God granted me some. David is the most athletic type of us all. He runs marathons and chops wood even when it's not stackable. He just likes physical challenges. This firing he so-called started on his own two days ago fits entirely within this perspective. There was no obvious urgency, at least not to me, in glazing that loaded collection of dried clay artefacts, although he said humidity would jeopardise the fragile solidity. A paradox I didn't really grab, fragile solidity. Nature is built on paradoxes.

They had just planned it all, he and his summoned soulmates. The pots had been assembled and stacked, but then came the rains and the flooding, persuading his firing companions to retire. And there he sat, with his loaded kiln and soaked matches.

'It's Aoife, for goodness' sake! Showing her boobs to David!'

Elizabeth has always been a swift and accurate observer, although her objects of inquiry don't actually require any swiftness whatsoever. Mushrooms don't exactly run off. They just appear. Unannounced, standing patiently still until further notice. It might be telling, but none of us really hunt speedy objects down. The only exception might be Boris, from Elizabeth's weird point of view. Pursuing the undaunted, never-ending traces of history and present. I think we all learnt how to immobilise or when to approach our objects of research comfortably. I just exploit my moths' morning numbness, to be honest. So does Georg with his sleeping dormice. I get more and more convinced of us being lousy manipulators. Lousy lantern lurers.

From afar we see Aoife faintly assisting David feeding the raging dragon, like a cheap pin-up model joining a coal dusted sweaty stoker keeping the Flying Scotsman pumping. Not the most successful metaphor, as I don't see steam or any moving mechanism, but the kiln holds a similar frightening power.

'The hot odd couple!'

Elizabeth's voice has switched tone and colour. The telling scene must have affected her as well. Although, I've never been able to accuse Elizabeth of really lusty articulations or behaviour whatsoever. She incorporates the indigenous reserve capacities and I fully blame her strict British upper class upbringing. She IS gorgeous and she's smart enough to have full awareness of it, but she doesn't exploit it. At least not openly. Frankly, I haven't been able to outline her in an acknowledged female category of mine, but that's perhaps more due to my lack of experience with girls and my fragile social network. I even doubt whether these last words picture the situation correctly.

'They wouldn't expect us here, would they?'

'Aoife saw me leave,' I say. 'That's for sure. And there's the habitual superficial distant waving with David when I pass. They must expect us somehow. At least David does.'

'Weird profiling then, don't you think?' Elizabeth mumbles. A clear pause signals a sincere thinking process, which most likely weighs several romantic plot options.

'Would they be in love?' she finally asks.

'Or just awfully hot.' I answer. 'That monster easily reaches one thousand degrees Celsius.'

'No, I mean why would she help him this way?'

'Because a dendrobiologist can?' I guess. 'She has plenty of time. Trees take their time, so do their observers. And I heard she needs the scaffolders to reinforce the concrete foundations of her scaffoldings. Mr. Lyndon padlocked the towers to prevent any hazardous access. So boredom perhaps, again? If you ask me, the rain must drive her mad. How many days have passed without real sunshine? Nearly a month? I still don't know why she keeps herself grounded on this sun forgotten hill.'

'Perhaps because I asked her?'

'You did? Why?'

'Because I didn't want to be the only girl, perhaps. And because Aoife and I… Oh, just leave it,' Elizabeth sounds suddenly irritated. 'I think I don't owe you any explanation. Moreover, I doubt whether you would understand. Let's just see what happens if they notice us. Shall we sneak up on them?'

'That won't be too difficult. David is always so focused on his flames.'

'Of course he is,' Elizabeth grabs her bosom with both hands and wiggles her elbows slightly. The hydrophobic fabric wrinkles funnily between her fingers but never reaches the perfect breast curves I'm secretly picturing whenever we meet. I give in by the sight of it all and laugh out loud again, fully overwhelmed by this unnatural posture.

My squeak must have alarmed the two dragon feeders, since they alter pace and posture abruptly, without any other obvious reason in sight. Aoife even disappears for an instance to emerge a bit later from behind another neatly piled portion of logs, her upper parts swiftly covered with some cheap white fabric. She still struggles, pulling her long hair out of the collar and mastering her molested pony tail back into an acceptable shape.

I hope our accidental intervention won't disrupt David's temperamental dragon, but Elizabeth is unstoppable now. She has resolutely taken the short cut across the field, straight towards the kiln, not realising she might ruin the fragile processes hidden within the short-tempered monster. From the first friendly tea spoon twigs to the three feet long robust planks of birch. Uninterrupted generous offerings to the increasingly demanding flames, raising the upcoming heat like a caring parent who does his best to rear a badgering teenager, but gradually, when heat reached independence and character, he gets completely baffled by the growing powers he's awoken.

David has more than once shared these parental metaphors at the hill table whenever explicating firings, but his narrative mostly has an adverse effect on the commensals, who are still sporadically cherishing doubtful adolescent behaviour themselves. Myself included.

Unfortunately, the dear consequences of these temperamental inner outbreaks are only observed when the harm is long done, when flames have disappeared and dust is professionally rinsed away. Remedies seem foolish and expensive, considering the spiking gold price and the much overrated kintsugi workshops in posh mindful circles. Modest David mostly blames his own amateurish human handlings in front of the feeding hole during the marathon battle. That cramped square metre confinement he's condemned to is crammed with traps of nasty trivialities and fatigue. Cherishing the idea he can fully master the wonderous world inside, makes him nervous and perhaps a bit idle too.

When we're quite close, we can actually feel the heat. I suddenly consider he too might be nothing but another hilltop chaser.

'I didn't expect you yet. You're early,' says David closing the kiln by shifting the tile lid back in front of its mouth. He takes off his enormous gloves and wipes drops of sweat out of his eyebrows. His wet T-shirt reveals his chest muscles and makes him look like an oiled gladiator during battle.

'I got some assistance along the track,' I confess, doubting very much whether Elizabeth would really have made the difference. I guess I just didn't linger at my usual potential points of natural interest.

'And the assistant seemed quite adaptive,' I add after a short pause, anticipating with a vain blinking at Elizabeth, 'cooperative and eager to learn, which makes all the difference.'

'And the evening delivered you some helpful backup too, apparently,' Elizabeth intervenes firmly by pitching the amicable tone to a higher, inquisitive range. She throws a weird, aggressive glance in my direction, nanoseconds after my missed wink. I don't really understand why, as I didn't want to sound patronising at all.

'And is Aoife as inquiring as I seem to be?' Elizabeth's voice is still climbing.

'Very inquiring,' shouts Aoife, appearing from behind the kiln, delivering and dropping a new ransom of planks for the next feeding session dangerously close to our feet. Like making a clear defensive statement.

David smiles gratefully. He winks in his turn successfully in Aoife's direction while she straightens her back and deals with a painful sting at the bottom of her spine by rubbing both hands intensively against her back muscles, just above her buttocks.

'We're nearly reaching the summit,' says David sternly, clearly unaware of the mutual parrying. 'The magical 1200,' he clarifies. The glazing finish!'

'Of course, the glazing!'

Elizabeth is teasing, skimming any tension between the two sweaty creatures, lured by some ignited fire within.

I just know she is. The way she is holding her head in this awry angle and the slower pace in her voice to feign some sort of interest and understanding. I'm honestly relieved she quickly redirected her sweet harpoons onto someone else. Her eyes bounce from David's chest to Aoife's and back again. The deposited wood has left dirty stains on Aoife's striped T-shirt and my eyes stick to an embarrassing rip close to her right nipple. I conclude for myself nobody has noticed it so far and I can't decide to tell the others or not.

'Are you taking the piss out of me?'

Lack of sleep has turned easy-going David cranky. I see Elizabeth being as surprised as I am. Also Aoife is silenced by that sudden rather violent outbreak.

'I'm not going to lecture on the crucial processes you're about to ruin with your invasive visit,' David utters annoyed.

Bad timing. Nothing but bad timing I silently say to myself. Aoife too mimics we'd better leave.

'I'm sorry, master dwarf, I didn't know you were forging precious metal,' Elizabeth suddenly bursts from behind the low wooden barrier. 'We just wanted to say hello. That's all. We even considered helping you in reaching any summit, but I guess we only have a cooling effect on the whole company. So we better leave you in peace. Forging bonds is a serious business. Come on, Bernie, before one of your rare night moths gets caught in these hellish flames.'

'What are you talking about, woman?' David sounds puzzled, not interested in arguing or whatsoever. 'We're not forging anything.'

I'm surprised by Elizabeth's villainous outburst. Calling David a dwarf is so unreal. He's not even the smallest of the pack.

'You jealous pathetic bitch!'

Aoife gets triumphantly before her. She is blocked by some badly fallen logs. Fortunately, I would think, because she sounds more arrogant than she did with Boris. The solid looking sisterhood that was forged at the promising dimming of this dying day, doesn't even stand the daring night. The dwarfing is perhaps a sensitive inside issue between both ladies. They might have been exchanging innocent jokes about measurements and heights, imagining along in playful terms and challenging biometrics. Forging seems indeed a tricky business. There's a truth in David's words. That when you play godlike games, you face awakening powers you cannot even dream to master and you become a helpless vessel bobbing behind a harpooned species. It is sound and clear that at least someone got hurt. Probably more than one. According to this same David, it's only a matter of sitting out and having finished what is started. And praying no great pots have been broken. But shards bring good fortune, don't they? I must give in that my thoughts get stuck somehow.

Elizabeth has already left the shelter, but she is heading the wrong way, diverging from my last unignited moth trap.

'Elizabeth, wait!'

I automatically run after her, like a loyal dog, worried about the wrong turn taken along its daily stroll. I feel myself chasing her, only after a short 'sorry' addressed to the pink sharp nipple piercing through the cheap fabric, hardened and reaching out for any consolidating revenge. I don't know why I apologised, but it just felt the least I could do. If it only were to account for my swift and cowardly desertion.

That night the tawny owls are surprised by two mysterious but joyful cries, resounding awkwardly through the silent woods. Competing one another with vengefulness and lust. I lack every scientific accuracy to confirm the true synchronicity of the two. Only later, when our trembling wet hands finally light the last moth trap, I acknowledge to my devastating astonishment the insignificance of it all. Descending all by myself, I try to disbelieve the painful truth, but Elizabeth's unforgiving pace leaves no room for doubt.

ACT IV

Water

'That is a lot of beetles in a box.'

I didn't expect Alan to be up already. Not that early anyway. My plan to sneak in the house unseen has failed, but giving it a second thought, I'm glad it's only him in the kitchen, stirring his northern version of porridge to save milk for worse times. The sugar is clearly an accession to the rationing. A crystallised spoon lies like a silent witness on the counter. It will unmistakably lead to tiring remarks on basic hygiene, clean kitchen tools and dry sugar pots, if it doesn't get cleared in time. Before the others arrive, that is.

'They're not beetles! They're moths!' I say.

'Of course they are, Ludwig.'

Alan has turned his back to the sink, suggesting he will most likely ignore the upcoming hygiene issue.

'I'll reflect on that,' I respond annoyed. I cannot count the times people have used this lousy pun when dealing with entomologists carrying boxes all over, even those with glass lids and the undeniable truth fixed underneath. It's so tiring when people keep showing off with their painful erudition. Certainly at this early hour. It's an academic characteristic, I suppose. And for what Oxford is concerned, one should quadruple it.

I'm about to put my nightly loot on the kitchen table. I'm holding the large wooden birthday cake box with both hands, till I know it's safe to loosen the grip. I recovered it from a retired biology professor. I believe it's a cake box because I cannot imagine hats being that big. He kept his old microscope and lenses in it. I hammered out his little home-made shelves and holders to make the egg cartons fit.

I honestly don't have the faintest idea what the outcome of the previous tumultuous night will be. Alan is perhaps right, in a way, mocking about with Wittgenstein. For me, I mostly balance my expectations between precious and common, but considering the others' facial expressions and lack of genuine interest, they mostly value it less. It's all in the hunter's head, I guess, and the thraldom the quarry forces him into. The hunter gets hunted. Does that make sense?

My mind kept making circles all night and it was too early this morning to speak of dawn when I finally gave in to this propelling curiosity. I got out of bed and it is rather funny to say, but I felt the presence of my balls while urinating. It gave the morning this ominous vibe. A sudden concern about things you shouldn't be feeling, even though you know they are there. A bit like the awareness of ghosts, perhaps. Or fairies planting sanitary towels in the woods. When I sneaked down the wooden staircase, their nerving presence fortunately disappeared. I pulled on my wellies and started my notorious walk again, dauntingly counting on the extraordinary.

If it only were for a faint echo of last night's disruptive proceedings. I had been trying to capture the most invasive aberrations in my logbook, still too excited to turn in, just to consolidate any accidental successful recipes for future lightings, but the mental print of the arousing touch of Elizabeth's naked body kept overruling any other possible detail in my freaking memory. She had blasted my nerves.

She had pushed me on to the last unfolded plastic foil, next to Margaret's pimped nail polish lamp. On the Great Ash summit. Like a phoenix lighting up from a cremated love affair. She had ripped the buttons of her rain gear like a professional Chippendale, unzipped and lifted, unbuttoned and pulled down. My newly promoted assistant had suddenly taken over. Knowing where and how to handle, in pitch darkness. She pinned me on to the hilltop, with my back nailed to the ground, arms and legs spread wide. She treated like an experienced observer, to make me perform outstandingly, to have me displayed in the best thinkable position, nicely framed on her mantelpiece.

All that nocturnal excitement had obliterated every notion of sleep. I couldn't square the vicious thoughts and circular shapes that kept looping under my crane. Moreover, the fact that Elizabeth had disappeared before that final lighting, kept puzzling me all night. She hadn't waited, let alone helped me fixing my zip or finding my keys that had fallen out of my right pocket. And she even failed to lead me down the tricky, rooted hill path.

It now felt like a sudden unique encounter between an elusive wild creature and its persistent chaser. I only couldn't quite figure out who had been playing what part. I still have, though, great difficulty with neglecting the image of the bug who was accidentally picked up, got brutally inspected, but eventually thrown away, bruised and half squashed, for not being that extraordinarily rare after all. So I indeed finally decided to scrap some comfort in the proof of this magically weird night in hopefully even more magical findings between the egg cartons of my five lamps. The only gnawing nuisance that breaks down all magic is this mild itch in my groin. The flag incident should perhaps not be taken lightly.

'By the way, how's your whale, Captain Ahab?' I fire back to Alan, casting a similar doubting spell in his direction.

'Any news from her or has she vanished into thick water?' No Ludwig this time, but good old flexible William again. I can't even be bothered about the same intellectual narcissism. One needs to adjust the weaponry according to the attack, especially in the heat of battle, perhaps.

'Ho, Bernie, I was just joking,' says Alan soothingly. 'Didn't you have a good night? There was a lot of hooting in the forest. Those bloody birds drove me nuts. Did you hear it as well? You must have. You do sleep with open windows, don't you?'

I confess I do. Throughout the whole year actually. Without any wire netting, even in summer, much to the dislike of the others. It's a cheap way of passively attracting moths, frankly. Even they get accidentally lured by some thermal comfort of human presence. I suddenly recall Elizabeth's naked skin against mine, wet by drizzle, but not cold at all. Cooled, yes, but still invitingly warm. It funnily reminds me I still need to check the curtains. I'm a poor warrior. So easily distracted and pacified at the same time.

'I do like owls, actually,' I say, 'they calm me down. Their repetitive call comforts me.'

'Of course, I could have guessed.'

A spoonful of porridge suppresses a smile on Alan's face. His muscled buttocks now lean fully relaxed against the sink and his eyes drift to the distant horizon of the opposite Helvellyn poster. I try to read his thoughts, but the morning numbness leaves too many options open.

'I'm just showing some interest too, that's all.' I quickly add, imagining the impact of those British vessels on the chance of the whale's survival. Even if it were to prevent her from swimming into French waters, if their interference led to a beaching, I wonder if Alan would still be that thrilled, seeing that last living Leviathan die under doubtful nudging circumstances. I draw some weird parallels with my lousy traps, but I spot too many ifs in my reasoning that I doubt its solidity. In the meantime I pull the levers to unlock my moth case. The previous owner poorly mounted them himself to prevent the lid from opening while granting the old, disused cake box a lousy touch of fresh practicality and importance.

Alan keeps staring at the Helvellyn summit as if his thoughts are elsewhere. Far above newly defined sea levels and flooded eel valleys.

'I don't know what's going on,' he suddenly says, 'but every platform is only streaming people's drowning miseries. As if there's nothing else going on. I even dare to believe they've lost her.'

The pun of streaming and flooding flashes through my mind, but I relent.

'It looks quite bad out there. Everyone seems affected by the rising river levels. My dad has been up all night anticipating the inevitable.'

'Which is?' I ask curiously.

'Evacuation, what else?'

'Shouldn't you assist him then?'

While moralising Alan, I automatically mirror the question towards my own context and I honestly can't think of any lifesaving reason that keeps me here. Countless excuses, yes, but the numerous needs out there outweigh my personal endeavours here instantly, I'm afraid. Certainly on the short term. Moths can fly. They'll survive.

'I told him I was stuck on this hilltop, which is partly true, Alan confesses. 'He had of course difficulty with believing that and he didn't hide his disappointment, but I won't step into that corrupting emotional trap of his. Being the son of a immigrated Swiss volunteer doesn't automatically arouse the readiness to do the same, does it?'

Alan has lost his dreamy stare and is looking straight at me, waiting for any sort of confirmation. I recognise the burden of unfulfilled paternal expectations, so I keep poking that sparkling passion that dragged him away from his dad's magnetic fields and that keeps most of us on this hilltop eventually. Lousy verses I never actually wrote down but that I made up after days of struggling with my own father and A-levels come to life again. Rhyming combinations with excuses echo through the dialogue: refuses, abuses, confuses,... Silly teenage struggles that still sound relevant, as if we've never actually grown up and we obscurely escaped to this bohemian lifestyle for a higher mysterious goal.

'What if she beaches today, somewhere?' I say with the greatest empathy I can gather.

'Well, that's another story then. In that case, I'm off.'

'Would you really? But you've just said…'

'Don't preach, will you! Just focus on your bugs!' Alan says irritated.

'She IS beaching! They can't save her anymore.'

Aoife has entered triumphantly and marches straight to the fridge. She is wearing a new T-shirt. And a bra. When she opens the door, she hums an obscure melody. She looks longer into the lit refrigerator's interior than environmental tips advise. It looks like she is secretly scratching too. Or is that a rather bold interpretation, inspired by my own pulsing nuisance? To my next surprise, she finally takes the last milk carton out of the door shelf. Would she be converted by omnivorous David, I ask myself, while poor Alan isn't even aware of the change, nor my averted gaze. He's seems completely captivated by the tell-tale news.

'Is she? Wonderful!' shouts Alan.

'What do you mean, wonderful? That implies the poor girl is dead or dying?' Aoife poses realistically. She sounds combative. The morning ease has vanished completely. She closes the fridge and leans against its door, holding the carton in her hand. Weird creases across the lap in her T-shirt show me I was right.

'That's not the point,' Alan says, 'I know your leaves don't have brains, but my species does. It is, therefore, painstakingly logical it has to die before the brains can be harvested,' Alan defends.

'A dead whale is more interesting to you than a living one?'

'To be frank, yes. What do you think Bernie will do with his bugs?'

Alan points at me with his sticky spoon still in his hand. The two look at me judgingly. In bed I had decided to sedate the whole content of the cake box to fix the memorability of my Elizabethan night, even if the outcome is less than common and openly arouses, or better, confirms the looming doubt of all the effort. I'm happy I don't have a whole boat crew to convince, but only me, a self-centred, miserable moth man.

As I freeze predictably, they both agree that insects aren't whales and accept the silliness of the drawn comparison, making it perhaps even more painful for me. I feel set aside like a kid while Mum and Dad are arguing over the big things in life.

'How do you know anyway?' Alan avoids the ethical drama professionally, like he did with his father's request.

'It was just on my newsfeed,' Aoife replies.

'Do you know where?'

'Do you mean where I read it or where she is kicking her rusty bucket, dreading the expected agonising strain of international interest while making up her troubled mind on which side she might throw herself on the beach that would guarantee the most dramatic footage?'

Aoife opens the carton and lifts the container to her lips. She drinks voraciously as if David's firing prompted her some extra manly ferocity last night. She hesitates, still the carton to her lips, then drains the milk again, while snorting heavily, pacing herself to claim someone else's portion as well. I suspect Aoife playing a game with the sole goal to challenge Alan's patience and overexcitement.

'Where it last surfaced of course,' Alan responds like a silly, hungry lamb.

After another blokey drink, Aoife gives in teasingly, as if she doesn't know.

'I've already skipped it. I thought you knew. Anyway,' muffling a burp, 'are you happy with the south coast?'

'Oh, leave it,' says Alan annoyed, 'I'll check myself.'

He empties his bowl with two scraping spoons, dropping everything rather noisily in the sink and leaving the kitchen in a state to unleash a war, working down his sweet watery oatmeal leftovers.

'Ask Boris,' throws Aoife after him, 'he'll know. He has the connections. And the exact coordinates. It would be a unique opportunity to get there before anyone else does. Although, it would be tough for her to beach unnoticed.'

This last sentence addresses Aoife only to me and winks thereby victoriously before putting the milk back.

I remain silent and stare astonishingly.

'He asks for it,' Aoife defends, 'choosing sperm brains over conservation efforts. Come on! This is so macho. He's simply after more bloody academic credibility credits for some lousy brain surgery, rather than helping her out again in free fucking waters. You don't harm your moths either, do you, like any wise person would do?'

I really feel like a little child, being stuck to Mummy's side and hesitating to give in to her points of view, while a secret bond with Dad is forged, not just because you agree with him, but because you scent her unjust dealings.

'Of course, I don't,' I lie and decide to keep Margaret's unscrewed nail polish remover in the box until I'm alone again. I knavishly close the levers again hoping she doesn't stay too long. The smell of chemicals might turn her fuming. I count on her going to check up on David or to go back to bed to catch up on some sleep. She turns her back to me and starts rinsing Alan's bowl and spoons. Perhaps to clean her spotted conscience or to give herself the gratifying posture that avoids any painful eye contact. Anyway, the elephant in the room weighs down so much on both of us that nothing trivial stands a chance. At least for half a minute because I really want her out. I run through my lousy tactics and go for the nosy nuisance option. Again.

'How did David's firing go last night? Did he reach the required summit?'

I notice how suggestive I sound. Being a master in double speak herself, I strongly doubt Aoife hasn't picked it up either, certainly with the lack of sleep and what seems to be an itchy G-spot. She keeps rinsing the sweet spoon under the running tap. She's clearly started the day with new standards. Milk consumption, water spillage, and remorse. What else to expect apart from a contracted VD?

'Fine, until you arrived. What on earth were you doing there?'

'I have a moth trap nearby. I pass the kilns every night. It's nothing new. By the way, you saw me leave yesterday, didn't you?' I consider her asking about her sideshow performance at the kiln and a good shameless scratch under the table surface, but relent for both cases. Another proof in the list of many that I'm even less courageous with women.

'And what was Elizabeth's role then?' Aoife questions further. It's not benign Bernie who bothered her. How could he? He's the soft, neglectable Belgian entity of the hilltop. The silent background character, who gets lines when all the others have run out of wits and jokes. It's noble Elizabeth she's after.

'Was she the Lantern Carrier?'

Funny, but I think she actually was and perhaps still is to me, metaphorically then, but again I'm not willing to tell the whole happy ending story, let alone the scoop of my burning balls. Only that she joined me near the Sitting Sisters, out of sincere curiosity for what I was doing out at night, that she helped me out with lighting the lanterns as if we had been doing this for years, and that we were both surprised to find her at the kiln.

'O come on, Bernie, don't be so naïve. Genuine interest? Elizabeth? In your miserable night bugs?'

The tone of her voice jumped to a higher pitch, gradually, by every word, and cut deeper in the hardened tissue of my much beaten and fatigued mental scars than I expect. I suddenly feel uncomfortable, with the unchecked moth box before me on the kitchen table, holding a possible bleak, sedated outcome along with a bottomless, pitch black emptiness. Aoife rages on, as she is used to doing when being upset, ignoring any collateral damage while fuming.

'That high-class turkey just found herself a good companion to sneak up on me. She can't have it that I'm having something with David.'

'Are you? Wonderful, for how long? Congratulations!'

Georg walks in. In pyjamas, showing the last stretches of his notorious morning erections, deliberately or not, it ended up this way after issues on braless T-shirt breakfasting by the ladies. Making his own point of gender equality, but not really succeeding since the girls professionally ignore his capricious proof of manhood before the first drops of coffee seep through the filter.

'You're the last one who needed to know,' Aoife sighs.

'Sorry, too late.' Georg passes Aoife triumphantly and heads to the fridge.

'I thought we had to keep the milk closed till better tidings?'

'Aoife drank it,' I snitch automatically. For deliberately denouncing my moths as bugs, to start with. I feel the sweet glow of revenge in my veins and am surprised by its acute beneficial effect. The warm, overwhelming punch reminds me of Elizabeth's detailed account of an experimental consumption of hallucinating fungi in the summer. I suddenly feel I must talk to Elizabeth. To reassure her I believe to understand why she had done what she had done. And that I most certainly am able to forgive her. Even the glowing groin fevers, perhaps.

'That's typical,' Georg fires along, 'if precious vegan supplies run dry, we return to our good old demonised alternatives. What has made you burn your principles? The alarming idea of shortage?'

'Mind your own business, Georg. Why are you up so early, by the way? I thought dormice sleep most of the day? Same for your creatures, Bernie?'

She looks at me again, accusing me of something she is to be blamed for as well? I'm still petrified by her previous attacks and take her accompanied piercing gaze like a roasted camembert. Luckily Georg reacts and takes over.

'Alan alarmed me. He rushed quite rudely into Boris's room, without even knocking. He whaled into him until he finally revealed the exact location of that beached fish. Sorry, mammal. It sounded like he would kill him. Aren't we getting a bit too old for this?'

Georg pours himself a glass of milk and drinks so eagerly that an evoked gratefulness towards Aoife's dietary infraction cannot be denied. She just did what he hadn't dared to do, selfishly opening the last milk carton.

'If we're fooling ourselves with our own demons, why not doing it with others? Let's call it therapeutic,' Aoife states firmly.

The room instantly regains its much appreciated morning stillness. The emptiness you observe when one totters drowsily into a kitchen's nocturnal phase, with the morning birdsong organically integrating in the background. A genuine kind appreciation for this rare homely isolation, but you relent to surrender because of the awkwardness when being caught, all by oneself on a cold, darkened kitchen chair with no great excuse for that deliberate capitulation to inaction at the brisk dawn of a promising new day. The only difference now is that there are three people in that same mystical room, stunned by an undeniable truth and a slight hint of acetone for that extra clinical touch of proof.

Aoife's words sound so cynical that they knock me down on to that same hard-surfaced kitchen chair, where the odour of expired polish remover is even stronger. The generated clarity is overwhelming. Perhaps we all need therapy, tranquilizers, and well-targeted antibiotics.

'Therapeutic?' Boris ruffles into this stilled pool of thought, stirring the murky bed like an ignorant hippo claiming his place in the water and disrupting this unique, reflective effort.

'Alan's gone completely bonkers,' Boris continues, 'he ran into my room, switched on the main light, and forced me to show him the latest whale info. Luckily I had a new feed published before I went to bed, otherwise, I would have been killed by now.'

'You will get killed anyway, someday,' predicts Aoife, 'that's for sure.'

Boris ignores Aoife's allegation of his own corruptive nature, pulls the opposing chair from under the table, and gets seated. The belt of his cashmere brown-beige dressing gown is completely twirled up and twisted, clashing with the outstanding standards of the fabric and my inner striving for neatness.

'Who told him I would know more about this Moby Dick thing? Never push once the ball is rolling. Let the internet do its work. That's crucial, boys.'

Even if he taught an all-girls class, I think Boris would still address the group with boys. I don't know why he is so gender insensitive. I wonder how Elizabeth would frame this within Boris's fictional biography. Where is she, by the way? Would she still be asleep? She must have heard Alan's outrage? Or received perhaps a same sort of early morning wake-up call from down under?

'I did,' Aoife says.

'Well, thanks a lot. I'm most grateful.' If Boris shows gratitude, it's cast in irony.

'You're very welcome!' Aoife echoes.

'Is it a certain payback for yesterday's incident?' Only now, Boris grants Aoife a glimpse. As if he wants to show he's not afraid to look his opponent in the eyes.

'Would you believe me if I said no?'

'Probably not,' Boris answers, facing my box again and turning me more nervous, for he must have picked up the sharp intrusive smell of acetone by now. 'What I want to say,' states Boris, 'is that I didn't report any beaching myself! Someone else did. Did you?'

Boris looks at Aoife and Georg inquisitively. I'm not even taken into consideration. And I think I'm glad about it.

'No,' they both reply in unison.

'Then someone else must have inserted that rumour, which means he has…'

'Or she,' Aoife intervenes.

'Or she has taken over the feeding process, corrects Boris.'

'Is that serious?' asks Georg a bit concerned.

'Not necessarily. Anyway, I think Alan definitely needs therapy. Or an escape from this hilltop.' Boris explains.

'Well, it's really surprising how he's clinging to this silly thread so passionately. His eel frustration and the flooding have enhanced the whole process, as predicted.' Georg adds with cold resoluteness. 'Our hypothesis seems to work.'

Georg sounds like a behavioural scientist who is analysing the first results of a neatly set up experiment. Proving what, for God's sake? I witness a bunch of plotting bastards playing games with the minds of some truly dedicated people, probably mine included, and I conclude they all need therapy.

'The whole world seems to have lost grip. My Instagram account is exploding. Most people want to save the poor girl, even though she's reportedly beached and half dead. Look!' Boris has dug up his mobile from an inner pocket and is scrolling down the incoming replies.

'Especially since that same person insinuated a pregnancy,' adds Boris analytically.

'Pregnant?'

There's David. People are dropping in at the weirdest moments. Like in a cheap comedy. Misunderstandings and deceptions are all about timing. Time and place. And the prosody of things. If one can master that, one is making history.

Another silence. I see Aoife, Boris and Georg exchanging glances. There is a fragile secret to be kept by this threesome. A game of checks and balances is quickly played, but not quickly enough for David's impatience.

'Who is?'

David looks a bit worried at Aoife while heading straight to the sink, like a bulky constructor returning from a hard day's work, hoping to unravel the homely plotting he's been expelled from by wife, pool boy, and kids.

'Luckily only the whale is, Mr. Potter!' Boris snaps sharply enough to silence the soft-hearted David. Boris is clearly referring to David's so called eternal mating state Boris enviously acknowledged him into. Just by being his own virile self, David has never been quite unsuccessful with the ladies, unlike Boris's own pathetic playboy-wannabee character. Would Boris be hinting at their earlier kiln courtship? I don't think he knows. Aoife belches softly, clearly struggling with the consequences of her fresh revolutionary dairy diet.

The cashmere gown makes Boris look preposterous considering the white skinned body masses it's covering. In the eye of villainous beholder Boris, David was, is, and will always be a downsized simple potter. A stone digger who ignores the gems of gold, and only gets thrilled by the sticky clay The City is paradoxically built upon.

David loathes Boris's deceiving nature and he will probably leave the kitchen once his hands are cleansed. He will seek genuine comfort in his London Clay coloured department room that is stored with ditto artefacts and stones and books on rocks and surfacing strata.

'Good for her,' David answers back calmly, hardly assessing the kitchen scene while rinsing the last wilful stains of soot from his hands. 'Then that individual hasn't been that lonely after all, has she? Any idea where the dad is?'

Again the eyeing game. Aoife turns paler and retreats mentally. The others are frisking the unexpected plot twist that surely plundered Moby's rarity status. I see them overthinking the consequences of this weighty new chess move.

'Some local vet seems to have assumed pregnancy,' Boris summarizes from behind his mobile.

'Did he get his whole arm into her...'

'Georg, for Christ's sake!'

A sudden move of her torso makes Aoife leap out of the kitchen, hopefully to the only flushing toilet on this floor level at the other end of the hall near the front entrance.

'It's not a sheep,' scolds Boris, ignoring Aoife's sudden disruptive flight. 'This is a fucking whale!'

Gagging noises are backed by David's running water. The acetone is increasingly intruding. The first sunrays beam straight through the kitchen window and make me squint. I feel dizzy and a wave of mild nausea sweeps over me. I wonder why Elizabeth isn't showing up.

'Ophelia12, that's the one who started it.'

'Started what?'

Alan's back. This is getting so weird. And exhausting.

Boris startles from behind his feeds and acts like a caught teenager.

'The assumption of beaching and pregnancy,' Georg picks in again masterfully.

'One of the reasons why a female whale seeks for coastal waters might be pregnancy or the anticipation of a possible premature birth.'

'A polemic has emerged,' Georg explains further. 'Well, that's to say, a new camp has been formed, to save the baby whale by keeping the mother alive, at all costs, even if she is actually dying. And the situation is a bit polarising at the moment.'

'I've just picked up the rumour as well. If that's true, which seems very likely, that would be wonderful, I think. If we could keep the mother in a comatose stable condition, we might save the foetus and we could monitor both brains at the same time. That's beyond my boldest expectations. I want to catch the early train to London. Has anyone seen the bike? Or Elizabeth? They're both gone.'

Alan has metamorphosed into a freshly enterprising, energetic researcher. He has clearly got rid of his eel related burdens. He has emptied his crammed mental traps and released their slimy content for another goal, to me, much further than the Sargasso Sea, as I myself am assessing the very feasibility of Alan's whole whale enterprise from a simple realistic, and, why not, scientific point of view.

He is undoubtedly awarding himself with the belief to be doing great stuff, wearing the blinding invincibility cloak I wore myself a couple of hours ago. Poor Alan. I see Boris being fully recovered and gloriously glancing at Georg for the unexpected twist of the so called pronounced pregnancy.

'By the way, do you know Aoife is throwing up in the ground floor toilets?' Alan reports.

'She drank too much,' Boris informs.

'She drank milk,' I add, to anticipate the upcoming misunderstanding. The room is already crammed with too many illusory games. The smell of polish remover doesn't affect their glimmer even slightly. On the contrary. The chemicals erase the thinning line between imagination and the big bad world. And I don't know which one is worse. It all seems so much entangled, when I consider us just here around this very same contaminated kitchen table top. Birdsong offers a silent comfort, but Elizabeth's absence hammers louder and louder and hints otherwise.

'Anyway, I'm off. I can't wait for lower water levels or official confirmations of the actual beaching. If someone can tow her to a bay, we can secure her. The Channel is one big misty soup today, but tomorrow promises clearing winds and spells. So I'm off, even though no bobbing soul is interested. People on the phone even start insulting me when I urge them to forget their flooding issues for one tiny second. And college is ignoring my calls as well. But I truly feel I must go. Even if I have to walk to Pevensey. There's more than just rising water levels. I have a career to consolidate.'

'Swimming would be more appropriate,' supports Georg, 'anyway, good luck!'

'I just need the bike, okay?' Alan raises his voice. Frustrations are being built up again. He jerks around like a hyperactive, fractious toddler. He even cancels his obligatory morning cappuccino, despite the unexpected frothed milk option.

'Who used it last?' Alan eventually shouts.

The others play an embarrassing statue game. Even David keeps washing his hands. I finally give in. After more than five uneasy seconds.

'If it's not under the oak tree, I don't know.'

'Why do you think Elizabeth took it?' I add inquisitively, more eager to dig extra information about Elizabeth than to smear an extra layer of soothing balm on Alan's weary soul.

'I don't know. Seems logical. No one else apparently knows and she's not here.'

As no one else really responds, and David even pushes him aside to reach the towel, Alan breaks and leaves the kitchen furiously.

'Thanks for the support!'

A grenade of reproach rolls underneath the kitchen table into the most remote, unreachable corner of the room, unable to cause substantial harm to any of the targeted.

'Don't forget your fishing rods,' shouts Boris behind him, and with that, another missile is being launched, all the way to Pevensey.

The silence strangely returns, only so different than before. More awkward than ever, like a suit that doesn't fit the party.

'Look what I found, Bernie, an exploding whale! Spaffing billions of rotting belly waste particles over this poor man.'

I loathe the lack of empathy. The craving of mastering. The mockery. This survival of the wittiest.

'Does that whale really exist?' I finally ask.

'Are there real beetles in that stinking box of yours?' Boris bites back.

ACT V

Thunder

'Poor girl' had been Alan's final words before he ended his voice mail, very uncomfortably, being completely taken by the stocked emotions. He clearly didn't really know how to deal with the devastating news. It is difficult to imagine her beached, but the resemblance is striking. I see her white flesh fully bloated.

I still hear Alan's clinical voice through Georg's phone speaker in my head, hardly audible because of the surrounding rustle of the Great Wood trees. It keeps playing like a giant loop. Constantly telling of the recovered bike in the flooding river. I try to get a grip on this appalling repetitive narrative, but things get so mixed up that I lose order and logic. My fingers are soaking wet and the more I fiddle, the dirtier things get. I have lost control entirely. I feel trapped and sedated.

'Poor girl!'

I simply can't remember why, but I proposed Georg that same morning in the kitchen to help him emptying

Alan's traps. I guess partly because I was afraid to face any disappointment in the content of the moth box and I desperately needed some sort of distraction from the anxiety concerning Elizabeth's disappearance. Anything would do. So why not that meek assisting with checking on Alan's traps. Elizabeth had helped me out as well, hadn't she?

'Poor girl!'

Elizabeth had left the hilltop, that's a fact. We checked her lab room and found the bed unslept in. The impressive old closet with hundreds of labelled drawers delivered one of the deepest and richest aromas I had ever smelt. It holds her massive collection of dried fungi. The specimens and samples are neatly categorised. The range is enormous, the variety breath-taking, but it looked only but a silenced witness, numbed by an extinct language, like an illegible account of an extended, multi-layered biography we were hardly aware of. It was like entering an old castle kitchen after an exuberant banquet. How different from the chalet's dining area, being poorly bleached by cheap aggressive acetone. Her workspace felt overwhelming and welcoming at the same time. A mysterious world that was only hinted at by a diversely perfumed autumnal air.

'Poor girl!'

'We just empty the traps, that's all, OK?'

That was Georg shouting from the hall. He was still negotiating the stern character of his boots while I was already outside underneath Aoife's shuttered windows. The morning was chilly but the sun had already cleared the mist under the canopies. The weather promised poor Alan at least good hopes of a clear and reflective sunset at the Channel, I thought. That was perhaps the only definable reason why I had decided to help Georg. To not ruin everything. To give Alan at least something to fall back onto. Vicarious shame, let's say.

'What about the figures then?' Which always seem to me more important than some distorted rusty fishing baskets.

'Don't you worry. I got my instructions. You don't have to do anything illegal, Saint Bernard.'

Georg got to his feet and stamped his squeezed heels in the required position.

'Come on then!' he shouted and set off, before I would change my mind, it seemed. He walked like a farmer, with massive steps. He treated me like a sheep dog who would be happy to be considered useful.

Georg chose the shortcut to the river and headed straight towards the Great Wood. I noticed he was not used to climbing and I caught up with him before we reached the mild summit. I stalled on the top and he didn't protest at all. He found support in a solid beech and overlooked the valley.

'Ahab dies in the end, doesn't he?' I heard myself suddenly say.

'Everybody does eventually, don't they? Who the hell is Ahab?' Georg was breathing heavily.

'The Moby Dick character. The captain of the Pequod. I think he dies at the end of the story and Moby Dick survives, doesn't he?'

'What the hell are you talking about? Has this acetone affected your brain or what?' gasps Georg, 'I'm trying to track these eel traps and you flirt with fictitious characters and whales. Grow up, Pinocchio!'

'Says who!'

'A twinge of remorse, Bernie?'

'At least someone has.'

'Oh, come on. We're saving Alan's career!'

'By bringing in false data.'

'Predictable data, that won't affect the outcome at all. Alan would not have left us otherwise, if we hadn't proposed to sub. And considering the situation now, he clearly wouldn't be able to recover the traps as well. And we give it at least a try.' Georg talked with great pauses. Like my grandfather had done on the day before he died.

'Just as he would have done,' Georg continued, 'and we will deliver additional footage of the flooding river to prove the gravity of the whole situation and to underline the finiteness of our efforts.'

Gravity and finiteness indeed. The great struggle of Man. The Great Wood seemed unforgiving for Georg, but he soldiered on in his defeat of the hilltop.

'What's wrong with a good laugh, Bernie? I would pay millions to see Alan showing the puzzled locals that footage inquiring where his giant whale has landed.'

A majestic River Thames claimed the lower grasslands with an unseen obviousness. The sunny spell delivered a stunning view. From this distance, the situation looked peaceful. The river flowed deceivingly naturally under our feet, as if it had always done so. We could clearly define the river bed according to the lined up canopies along the flooded banks. It felt weird to behold the oh so familiar valley altered. The raised water levels had reshaped the look of the valley. And the sound. As if an unbeatable argument was uttered in the grand debate. The river had suddenly spoken and silenced everything.

Georg dug up his mobile to check the digital map on which Alan had marked the traps. He was looking for any tributaries and a bridge.

Georg had settled himself under some hazels on one giant root knob. The bearings were still puzzling him. He kept turning his device and reading the landscape, until he noticed Alan's voice mail. He listened to the message himself, multiple times. Holding the device quite close to one ear and closing the other with his other hand. The message got overruled by the gentle breeze playing with leaves in the majestic trees around us. He then turned on his speaker and pulled me down under the same hazels. He clearly didn't want to bring the news himself.

'Poor girl!'

An escaped Moby Dick sounds ridiculous nowadays. It would simply be unthinkable, inexplicable and shameful perhaps as well, with all the tools, data and knowledge we've acquired over the centuries, to let a giant creature simply slip through our fingers. We don't even need giant species, even if there were still any left. We create our own precious untamed monsters if necessary, building our own unexplored islands and jungles, with beneficial motives and scary demons. And we grow more professional than poor old Ahab. We chase more effectively because we're no longer stopped by any limping or lousy vessels, nor by ignorant crew members. On the contrary. If they rebel, we inform them, alternatively. We consider the whole wide range of possibilities and the vast powers that they generate. It has become so embarrassing to face defeats, that we choose our winning battles constantly. And afterwards, we safeguard our miserably achieved victories by distinct borders.

'Poor girl!'

I see David and Aoife from the glade on the flank of the hill, instructed by Alan, standing along the flood line in the distance. In colourful raingear, even now when the sun is shining. But it all makes sense. The water is omnipresent.
Then I suddenly spot things glittering, probably some spokes and the round wheel hub stuck halfway above the

water level, down in the valley, quite close to the flooded road across the grassland, stuck against some bushes.

I've never shouted that loud in my whole life. Its primal character startles Georg to his feet and silences him for the next ten minutes. I lead him downhill, out of the woods, to the waterline. He is the one who's following now. I take the path downwards that seems zigzagging endlessly through the hillside forest. I try to keep my eye on Alan, David and Aoife, but again muddy roots hold me back. In every bend I stop to look up and check up on them. They're moving further away from the bike, downstream. They look like tiny flashing road markings channelling the currents safely passed the obstructing lower banks. Three courageous matchstick men, sticking out and bordering the treacherous torrents. I lose sight when we reach the canopies of the lower trees, and the path gets even soggier and more slippery, slowing me down and upsetting me even more. Georg is doing his best to keep up. It's more like running, perhaps, although we both hardly understand what's actually pushing us. Good old gravity, for sure, to name at least one.

I can't get the image of a beached Moby Dick out of my head. I hardly grasp the devastating impact of this alternative plot twist. The mind-blowing sceneries of this flooded valley pound my saturated soul like cheap metaphors and feed the numerous narrative waves that keep crashing nearly simultaneously down on me. Harpooned or not, but undoubtedly nudged, by all means. I'm a bit bold with timings, motives and topics, so do forgive me, but I sense one undeniable shaded mantra prophesying gloomily about a fading magic. I hear it humming constantly while descending. The majestic entity the whale was famously hunted for, lies stretched and wrecked on a pebbled soil. It is dying, putrefying, rotting, decomposing, and evaporating until nothing but an inconvenient carcass remains, resembling not in a billion years the bespoken grandeur it once had. It is this massive sadness that keeps sticking to my nerves.

Icy water suddenly gushes into my boots. The cold paralyses my thinking. I'm convinced of still being on the road, heading towards the passage between the two parallel bridge rails the current is now flawlessly crossing. The hierarchy has changed. The world has changed.

'Bernie, come back, you fool! It doesn't make sense.' Georg shouts a couple of feet from behind. He sounds worried and panicky.

'It looks like we've found the bike. Look!'

He points to my left and indeed, about fifty yards downstream I see the wheels much more clearly now, struggling with any surrendered floating artefact, like poorly tinkered eel traps. I see Georg approaching. His legs halved by the water. He stretches his arm towards me.

'Come on, Bernie. What do you want to prove? There is a safer way. Come, take my hand.'

'Poor girl!'

We go straight to the willows, across the flooded grassland. The current is weaker and the soil surprisingly less soggy than expected. We are skimming the nervous waterline on both sides of the river, in search of a body hiding unnaturally beneath the water surface, amongst the many leaves and twigs and branches, hopefully still drifting amongst the massive amount of debris in the majestic bend that might hold her in this painful corner of the world.

'It's all my fault.' Aoife sobs dramatically. Her face even more pale than when Georg glued her to half a bottle of vodka in the kitchen. It's his notorious Russian remedy for stomach problems.

'No, it's not,' tries David, but he realises his words aren't convincing.

'I think we all are a bit responsible,' Georg adds, trying to turn the appalling idea bearable by dividing it into smaller parts, but it has a reversed effect. It multiplies massively and contaminates the five of us, like a contagious sickening virus, bringing us down to a numbing fever of guilt and impotence. I don't really acknowledge my personal contribution to this horrid outcome yet, but I accept the massive burden remorsefully, just like the feverish itch that keeps pulsing in the base of my belly.

Sauced Aoife nestles herself against David's torso while we four stare over the currents, skimming the borders in search of a log-like entity that once was the astonishingly beautiful Elizabeth.

'It was just a silly game. Between girls.' Aoife suddenly mumbles. She needs David to find balance in the soggy soil. Her slurred words sound like a lousy confession, perhaps an apology as well. Anyway, at least an embarrassing attempt to deal with this irreversible past. Or is it? Where is Boris? Where is our historian when you need him?

'About a week ago, Elizabeth and I were just prattling away, like two foolish teenagers,' Aoife continues. 'We had been nibbling at some mushrooms, which we occasionally did. She has this dried collection, you know. "The green bag", as we would call it. It's always just jolly good fun.'

Aoife smiles funnily. She seems to be doing her utmost best to frame herself in some sort of way, but the mitring fails completely. As if she could wash her hands in the abundance of water running along our feet, draining the sticky muck from this miserable boggy outcome.

'I remember we cheered a lot and tattled the time away. We even talked about first boyfriends. Typical girls' stuff. And then suddenly, we came to the flooding and the silly idea that what if the isolation lasted forever and that we were condemned to each other for the rest of our lives. I mean, just the seven of us. It was just … it was just silly!'

Aoife gets emotional and starts sobbing. Tears are running over her cheeks now. It's all getting very theatrical. I don't know where she's taking us.

'Who would we choose? That was the question. Her question, actually,' Aoife stresses.

'She was really after this. And I just played along. We took post-its and wrote our number one down. Secretly. We counted to three and stuck it on each other's forehead. That's when it all started, I guess.'

There's a slight hesitation now. She holds her breath and looks at David. The river keeps flowing resolutely. Unstoppable. The look of this constant majestic streaming is unsettling. There seems no room for details, but Aoife attempts to save some from drowning.

'We had both picked David,' she nearly yelps, 'which we immediately laughed away of course. We admitted it was a matter of elimination, like two crazy schoolgirls weighing five boy band members.'

Aoife pauses again and presses herself more firmly against David, but he remains motionless. He is probably too surprised by the sudden inconvenient truth and the perhaps even more painful nomination of a cheap teenage idol. He is not echoing Aoife's emotional outburst, nor answering her sudden need for comfort. But he is scratching too. Discreetly, but he is.

'Then Elizabeth asked whether I had considered her for one bloody second. It was a weird question. I had seen the game from a procreative point of view,' babbles Aoife further, 'so I said no. And if I had, it wouldn't have made a difference. Honestly!'

It seems like Aoife keeps checking her own credibility or she is fighting the alcohol? We keep staring at the impressive current and the rapid movements of things passing. Her words take off as well, instantly. Downstream. And I hardly realise the true impact of it all.

'And then she suddenly came up with this crazy coupling bet. Sorry, guys, but it looked all very innocent and silly. It really was, at least for me. And I thought a bit of flirting wouldn't harm the hilltop boredom at all, would it?'

She is addressing herself. Georg has left the spot we are standing. It's clearly getting too personal for him.

'Elizabeth seemed quite serious about it. She definitely wanted to test me. Or her own gorgeous self. I just know. She always had some challenging superiority about her. Constantly pretending silly excuses or reasons to feel sorry for her. All ridiculous bullshit. 'Cause there are none. None, you hear!'

Aoife talks as if Elizabeth is dead and I don't know why we don't deny it. David pushes her arms gently from his body and disentangles himself from her grip. Aoife is getting in overdrive. Fortunately, she doesn't resist either. There's no point of correcting or steering. Her story has reached the treacherous rapids as well. We let it flow. In the presence of a rusty bike and a missing envied aristocrat, so it seems.

'For myself, I was just curious to see how far virtuous Elizabeth would go, having made that daunting proposal herself. There was no real reward. Only the experience perhaps. And the detailed debriefing afterwards. We laughed again, all tantalized and stoned. And she sealed the challenge with this annoyingly lasting kiss. It was then that I tasted her flirting wickedness. I suddenly understood what she was really after. I presume…'

Aoife pauses.

'I presume Elizabeth fancied me and she wanted to make her point. That she herself was the best hilltop option I could think of. I cannot remember what happened afterwards, that evening! I really can't. I only woke up much later on the lab floor, still in pyjamas. Elizabeth had pulled the blankets from her bed to cover ourselves. I sneaked out before she would wake up. I didn't want anyone to find out. I felt uncomfortable and flattered at the same time. I couldn't be angry with her either. I just didn't feel right about things that probably might have happened.'

We all don't say a word. As a matter of fact, Georg has already outreached hearing distance, with the clear excuse of searching for Elizabeth. Too many details are being said. My male brain is trying to square the titillating scene with the appalling reality. Stop, Bernie.

'We didn't mention that evening again. I guess she couldn't remember the escapade herself, so I did as if nothing ever happened. But her challenge survived. Two days later, my original post-it was deliberately stuck on my desk for me to find it. David's name was crossed over. It was then that I started plotting myself. I relocated the flags. It was a cunning idea, actually. Clearly suggesting this venereal disease. Sneaky, but effective. It's only right to even out unequal standards. It gave me at least for once a bit of a lead in the challenge. And then I pointed my arrows at you, David. It was all very honest and sincere. It truly was. And when she caught us at the kiln, she freaked out completely, as you know, Bernie, because she took you into the woods. Didn't she, Bernie?'

As I don't really respond, Aoife continues. 'Victory was mine. I mean ours.' Aoife looks at David, but all in vain. The water keeps washing relentlessly and we sink more deeply into the saturated bankside.

And then they reluctantly reveal that Bernie got shagged under the Great Ash moon tree, because Boris's camera had streamed the footage on his moon tree account. It was the twelfth mating recording. #Spaffingbillions12. Mating it was. Like two nudged species, fed and tricked together, to breed if lucky.

'We need to go back to the chalet to call her family and the authorities,' says David, 'to report her at least missing.'

'Isn't that the same?' mumbles Aoife, but the alcohol has taken her too far to be taken seriously.

I pull my boots out of the holes I've been disappearing into and intend to leave. Run would be more appropriate, but the soil won't let me. I follow the whole track back. I grab the branches to pull me forward, hoping to reverse time. To keep the world from spinning in the direction it is brutally twisting. I want to go back in a pathetic attempt to rewind and undo what has been done.

'Poor girl!'

The kitchen table works contemplative, with all the others at a safe distance around me. I doubt they would fight the same image as I do, of a lamenting Ahab facing Moby Dick's bloated white body. The smell of acetone has been escaping from my intoxicating box ever since and has filled the room completely.

David didn't take his boots off. I like his pragmatism. Just boldly doing what is actually needed. He tilts one window and then goes quietly to the sink, inhaling the incoming woodland air, probably finding comfort in his much cherished view of the trees. Letting everything cool down, like his pottery in the sealed kiln. Patiently. But then he suddenly says: 'Spaffing seems your favourite word, Boris.'

A hostile tone. A sort of poking. Peeping. An impatient checking of temperatures. An underhanded accusation, even though David is not directly facing Boris. That makes it even uneasier to deal with probably.

'What are you referring to? The moon tree post? Is that it?'

'As a matter of fact, it is, yes.'

'Well, everybody has the right to claim his own moment of fame and glory. Just like Alan, no? And anyone else here in this room?'

'DOES HE?' David is clearly baffled. I have never heard him screaming that loud. I see a couple of birds fly off together. The presumption is quite rude indeed. Likely inappropriate. But perhaps inconvenient too. What was Boris actually insinuating? It's remarkable how calm he remains. If history has brought him anything, it must be an immunity for talking about dead or at least absent people.

'How dare you frame Elizabeth like that?' An unexpected remorseful outburst by Aoife. The walk to the hill has done her some good. 'As if screwing a Belgian was her long-awaited endeavour? This is noble Elizabeth we're talking about.'

'How dare you frame Bernie like that?' echoes Boris crisply. 'Why don't you react, man? Say something!'

I feel nailed down, pinned. Neatly stretched by the foulest of hands. Ready for display. It's the first time Boris is really advocating for me, but it feels more like criticism. The only moment he sounds a bit upset as well.

'What I'm trying to say,' says Boris, 'is that Elizabeth only has herself to blame.' He seems not affected by the many accusations and in the least by emotions. 'She knew exactly what she was doing.'

'Like I was, do you mean,' adds Alan. 'You made me believe there was this whale and you knew I would genuinely think I was the right person in the wrong place? That I would give in to my frustrations and that I finally would brainwash myself I HAD to leave? And that I would finally fool myself with the idea that everybody else would have done the same? Is that what you are saying?'

We are all facing Boris now, but he seems to know better. He knows we know. That we are all plagued by the same egocentric vanity which has us quarantined on this bloody hilltop island longer than we can imagine. He looks untouchable and he is clearly enjoying this.

'Why else would she have done it before the lamp got lit?' Boris explains. 'Bernie's lights blind the infrared camera as we all know. And she could easily have picked another location too. The woods are big enough, don't you think? It looks like I did her a favour. So don't blame me. I accidentally boxed some facts. Just like Bernie does with his stinking cake container over there.'

Elizabeth didn't know what tree it was, did she? I don't see why she would have lied about it? I try to recall her moon tree account. The words on our nightly walk in the woods, but "poor girl!" keeps flushing away any upcoming memory.

'When did you find out the whale was a hoax?' Georg asks Alan.

'That's not important now,' Boris prompts.

'I'm afraid it is.' Alan is leaning against the sink in exactly the same position as he did this morning, with his gaze focused on the magical Helvellyn poster.

'Elizabeth told me.'

'She did what?' Aoife shouts. 'When?'

'I got this text message just after breakfast,' he starts reluctantly. 'It said that the whale thing had been a complete setup. That she had just posted messages of a beached pregnant whale herself, to blow up the whole story. To teach you all a lesson, I guess. She was sick of this whole bloody hilltop circus. It's clear she wanted to help me. And I really appreciate her for that. She even instructed me to play along, to explicitly believe all that was still coming, the polemics on the beaching and the pregnancy, and to leave this place as soon as I could to keep your story going.'

'Do you realise Elizabeth might have killed herself because of you, Boris?' David and Boris get really close. The sight of the two men facing each other is scary. Each harnessing his own conviction and competence. Not much is needed for any form of aggression.

'What do you mean? Killed herself? She's not reported dead, is she? And what makes you say I killed her, David? She might as well have taken the rusty bike to fetch her morning-after-pill in town?' Boris objects.

'How do you know for sure?' David replies.

'How do WE know for sure?' Boris claims.

'STOP IT!' Aoife cries and weeps at the same time. This doesn't bring her back, does it? We just don't know anything.'

'Well, Elizabeth happens to be Ophelia12,' Alan continues. 'I couldn't really see the link, but I'm afraid I do now.'

'O my God!' Aoife panics. She seeks support in a cold Formica kitchen chair. We all watch her breaking down.

'But there's something else you need to know, Aoife. Elizabeth was worried about being pregnant. She secretly shared this concern some days ago, while questioning me about her flag incidents. I'm sorry to tell you now, David, but she said it was yours. She was about to tell you, but some things came in between, she said.'

'That's ridiculous. It's just impossible!' reacts David. 'It... It was just a flirt. Nothing more.'

'What do you mean, a flirt. So there was something?' Aoife asks inquisitively.

'Yes and no. I mean.'

'Yes or no, David?'

'Well, yes, but...'

'When?' Aoife is fuming. Her inner self is boiling over.

'What do you mean, when?'

'When, David? When did you fuck her?'

'I didn't, we didn't. Well, she started something, but it didn't lead to... you know. I was inspecting the kiln... It's impossible I made her pregnant.' David panics.

'And her ladyship was inspecting you. And then you felt you could start the siege and yes, why not loading her bloody kiln...'

'Come on, Aoife, please, it's not what you think...'

'What? Too many metaphors? You're just a sneaky bastard! I hate you!'

'What if she made it up?' Boris intervenes.

'What? Her pregnancy?' Georg says.

'Or the affair with David.' Boris adds.

'Come on, Boris, this is no beaching whale. Who would sell his own virginity?'

Georg harvests a weird sort of silence. People in the room need time to capture the impact of what he has just said.

And her death! I silently complete. In one giant relief. I suddenly understand. Thanatosis, of course. I feel a weird upcoming void from the inside of my brain. Like a convenient withdrawal from this miserable mishmash. Blanking out everything like when one plunges into deep water. I see Elizabeth's white legs teasing me deeper and further away from the rancid looking table surface. Like a new gracious white whale, of another kind and another world, depicting the embarrassing truth that we are failing and fooling masterfully.

'BERNIE! Wake up!'

They're all there, around the kitchen table. More concerned than ever. Alan, David, Boris, Aoife and Georg.

They lift my head from the cold and smelly Formica and pull me upright and help me firmly to my feet. They ask me questions, but I cannot answer any single one of them. I truly can't.

I spot my opened cake box outside and I see David finally emptying Margaret's unscrewed nail polish remover in the sink.

I realise I will never be able to prove the righteousness of that Elizabethan hilltop night. The kitchen lights burn into my eyes. They feel surprisingly warm and comfortable.

EPILOGUE

Dear Bernie,

When you read this, I hope to be in town, in a posh hotel bed in Oxford. In Malmaison's highest room I could book. The place where today's villains like me belong, perhaps. I just want to tell you I'm alright. Not drowned, nor pregnant, but safe, alive, and dry. It's just underneath the roof, so I will be safe for a while. Till the water level has dropped.

I'm sorry to have dragged you through this nightmare. If there is someone who doesn't deserve this, it's certainly you. I'm sure you can forgive me.

I wanted to make a point. I only hope that it really has shocked the others, although, I also believe that some people never change. It also forces me to make a new start, finally, because I've been making one big mess of my life so far. I am upset and awfully disappointed in people and things, and most of all in myself. I need a reboot. I silently count on the ability to thrive on rotting pasts. My mushrooms convince me daily I can, so I'm in good faith.

Consider our moment on the Hill as a genuine act of appreciation. I honestly grant you this happy ending moment. Cherish it. I don't regret it one second.

It is a goodbye in many ways. I desperately need some time for myself. To deal with my demons. The upsetting affair with Aoife triggered more than I could imagine. I need to settle with my past and my true orientation, to persuade myself to face the world the way I am. I fear the response of my family, the poorly proposed therapies, the expensive country retreats and the many labels they might stick on me, but I mustn't worry. I am who I am. And I want to cross rivers, even though they've never taught me to swim.

"It's not because they're called night moths that they're ugly." Those were your words, Bernie. We're so easily deceived by the way we look at things. They were a great eye-opener, just like your thanatosis-trick was.

Keep those lights burning, luring lantern lighter. And reveal the hidden world we constantly neglect. You never know I might surface again, one day.

Take care!

Your Ophelia12

PS: Good luck with that moth challenge thing. I think you deserve to win. You caught at least me and that's an outstanding achievement.

Acknowledgements

I owe this book entirely to the inspiring friendship of Robin Wilson and Rosie Fairfax-Cholmeley (Wytham Studio). This work would never have been written if I hadn't accepted the warm invitation to their linocut workshop in France in August 2019. It was the combination of the ongoing Brexit saga and their personal preparations for the Melville exhibition at the Bodleian Library on the occasion of the author's 200th birthday later that year that led me to the idea for *Wytham Whales*. I relate it all to those lovely creative moments on that sunny wooden bench in the Dordogne. Later, I had the opportunity to experience the same stimulating hospitality in Oxfordshire and I'm most grateful for Robin's vital guided tour through Wytham Woods (Oxford, UK).

www.ingramcontent.com/pod-product-compliance
Lightning Source LLC
LaVergne TN
LVHW041641060526
838200LV00040B/1668